"Kiss me," she said, and he did.

"Oh, God, Mae, I've wanted you," he whispered, and she opened her eyes to see him gazing down on her, his eyes black with desire. When he went to kiss her again, she stopped him, her hands cupping his face.

"Let me look at you," she murmured. "I can't believe it's you. I can't believe it's *us*."

"I wanted you the moment you walked into my office." He grinned at her. "In that damn pink suit." He rested his forehead on hers. "I can't believe it's us either."

"Make love to me," Mae whispered. "Make love to me all night."

He kissed her once more, a long deep kiss that made her body curve around his, and his hands moved, too, molding her to him. "Whatever you want," Mitch whispered back. "Whatever you want, Mae, you can have...."

Jennifer Crusie lives in a small Ohio town with four cats, three dogs, two mortgages and a teenager. She began reading romances for a university research project—and enjoyed them so much, she decided to try writing one. She not only *tried* but has succeeded! *What the Lady Wants* is Jennifer's fifth published book. Look for many more humorous, sexy Temptation romances from this talented author!

Books by Jennifer Crusie

HARLEQUIN TEMPTATION
463—MANHUNTING
480—GETTING RID OF BRADLEY
520—STRANGE BEDPERSONS

WHAT THE LADY WANTS

Jennifer Crusie

Harlequin Books

TORONTO • NEW YORK • LONDON
AMSTERDAM • PARIS • SYDNEY • HAMBURG
STOCKHOLM • ATHENS • TOKYO • MILAN
MADRID • WARSAW • BUDAPEST • AUCKLAND

This book is for my parents,
Jack and JoAnn Smith of Wapakoneta, Ohio,
because they gave me values, books and love

ISBN 0-373-25644-2

WHAT THE LADY WANTS

MAE SULLIVAN FROWNED up at the grimy old office building
and shifted from one aching spike-heeled foot to the other,
trying to keep the weight off her blisters. From the looks of
the neighborhood, her chances of getting mugged were only
slightly outweighed by the chances of the building falling on
her. Only a loser would work in a place like this.

Good.

She'd found her sucker: Mitchell Peatwick, private investigator.

It hadn't been easy finding an incompetent private eye on
such short notice in a midwestern city like Riverbend. She
couldn't exactly go around asking for referrals to stupid
gumshoes. So she'd started with the A's in the Yellow Pages
and worked her way down, rejecting one competent, prosperous P.I. after another as her blisters swelled and bubbled.
But now there was Mitchell Peatwick. She could picture him,
leaning back in his office chair, balding and overweight,
slack-jawed and beady-eyed, no brains to speak of.

He'd patronize her because she was female.

She'd play him like a piano.

All she had to do was convince him that he was investigating a real murder case, and he'd swing his paunchy weight
around, creating noise and confusion until whoever had
taken her uncle's diary would be forced to either give it up or
bury it forever if he didn't want to be accused of murder. Yep,
that was all she had to do. *So go do it*. She took a deep breath
and winced as the waistband of her borrowed pink skirt cut

into her flesh. Then she pulled the veil on her hat over her eyes and walked toward the cracked glass doors of the old building, watching her reflection as she climbed the steps.

Even through the dumb pink veil, she really did look sexy.

It was amazing what clothes could do.

Now, if she could just get this damn interview over with before the waistband of June's skirt cut her in two and June's heels made her lame for life, she'd be on her way to solving all of their problems.

Please let Mitchell Peatwick be dumb as a rock with a weakness for women in tight suits, she prayed as she rang for the elevator. *Please let him be everything I need him to be.*

THE WINDOW behind him was cranked wide-open, and the ceiling fan above him stirred the air, and Mitch was sure if he got any hotter, he'd die. As it was, he was pretty sure that the only thing that kept him alive was the fact that he wasn't moving. If he moved, his body temperature would rise, and he'd melt right there in his office chair.

He didn't want to move, anyway. He was too depressed to move. He leaned back in his cracked leather desk chair—sleeves rolled up, hands laced behind his head, heels crossed on his battered metal desk—and thought about the way he'd planned things and the way they'd turned out. Big difference there. Anticipation was a lousy preparation for reality. That's why he was giving up anticipation for fantasy. Fantasy was not particularly productive, nor was it lucrative, but it beat reality hands down.

Reality sucked.

Reality was leaving a prosperous career the year before on a spur-of-the-moment bet to become a private detective. Reality was regretting it. He'd envisioned himself as a lone knight fighting evil, the Sam Spade of the nineties. He'd since learned that being a private detective meant divorce work and more divorce work, occasionally relieved by more divorce work, and in most of those cases, as far as he could see, everybody was evil. Mitch hadn't had many illusions about relationships before, but he had absolutely none now. Even people who weren't married had him investigate to see if the people they weren't married to were telling the truth. And of course, they weren't. That was the one irrevocable truth Mitch had learned in a year.

Everybody lied.

Sam Spade would have understood that part, but he would have spit on the divorce work. Mitch had the uncomfortable feeling that he should be spitting on it, too, instead of making a precarious living at it. Too precarious. He had one week left in the year, one week to earn the last of the twenty thousand dollars and win his stupid bet and go back to his regularly scheduled life, but to do that he needed a client who would shell out $2,694 before Friday.

It wasn't going to happen. Prying money out of clients was the second least favorite thing he'd learned about this job.

So when he heard the elevator cables rumble in the hall opposite his office door, he didn't leap to his feet with enthusiasm. It wasn't just because the heat would kill him if he moved. It was also because it had been a long time since he'd done anything with enthusiasm, and he'd forgotten how it worked.

If I was Sam Spade, this would be Brigid O'Shaughnessy. The ancient ceiling fan creaked above him, and buttery sunlight spattered over him, and in spite of himself, he began to feel optimistic again. Maybe hope wasn't dead yet. Maybe this was Brigid O'Shaughnessy heading his way, after all, a woman uninterested in marriage and commitment, willing to seduce him to get what she wanted.

He was sure as hell willing to be seduced.

She would come into the office, cool, slender, lovely and lethal, in one of those white suits with the wide lapels and a tight skirt that was slit to the hip. She'd have incredible legs. And maybe she'd be wearing a hat over her glossy red curls, a dark veil that dusted over blue, blue eyes and a straight little nose above moist, pouty lips. And in between the lips and the legs would be the best part. Her jacket would be tight under her breasts. Round breasts. Full, round breasts. High, full, round breasts.

With an effort, Mitch moved his mind away from the breasts.

And she'd come in and say, "I need you to find the Maltese Falcon," and her voice would be throaty and soft. And somewhere along the way, she'd take off her hat, and they'd have passionate, steamy, slippery, sweaty sex . . .

Mitch lingered for a moment on the sex.

. . . and then he'd find out that she'd been the guilty one all along. "I won't play the sap for you, baby," he'd say, and they'd take her away for murdering his partner. Okay, he didn't have a partner unless he counted Newton, and nobody ever counted Newton, but still. . . . No wonder that book was a classic. Sam Spade got to nail her without a commitment and still feel good about himself when he dumped her. First, great sex, and then he walked out on her, free as a bird, a hero instead of a schmuck.

Now *there* was a fantasy.

Then the door opened, and he looked up, and she came in.

Her hair was dark brown, and so were her eyes behind the veil, and her suit was pink instead of white, but everything else was pretty much his fantasy. The nose, the lips, the . . .

"I'll be damned." With enormous effort, Mitch raised his eyes from her breasts to her face.

"Probably." Her voice reverberated straight into his spine. "Are you Mitchell Peatwick?"

"Uh, yeah." Mitch swung his feet to the floor and stood up, wiping his sweaty palm on his shirt before offering her his hand. "Mitch Peatwick, private investigator. Listen, did you ever read *The Maltese Falcon?*"

"Yes." She ignored his hand as she surveyed the dingy office, her pout deepening as she took in the cracks in the upholstery and the dust. "Is this really your office?"

Okay, she wasn't impressed with the accommodations. And obviously not with him, either. Well, that was the way the world worked. Anticipation tripped him up every time. If she'd just kept her mouth shut, she would have been perfect, but no . . .

Reality. Nature's downer.

Mitch sighed and pulled his hand back. "Think of it as atmosphere. I do." He sank into his chair and put his feet back up on the desk. "Now, how can I help you? Lose your poodle?"

She quirked an eyebrow at him. "Would you be able to find it if I had?"

"Just what I needed—a snotty client." Mitch tried to keep the annoyance out of his voice, but it was hard. There was something about being snubbed in the middle of a heat wave by a beautiful woman with fantasy breasts that brought out the worst in him. And anyway, she wasn't that beautiful. Her nose was actually pretty standard, and her lips didn't really pout on their own, and her breasts . . . *Don't think about the breasts,* Mitch told himself. *It'll only depress you.*

"From the looks of things, you could use any kind of client." She surveyed the bottoms of his feet, propped up on the desk in front of her. "I've never actually seen paper-thin soles before. It's amazing. I can tell the color of your socks from here. They have holes in them, too."

"Big deal." Mitch smiled, world-weary and invulnerable. "Now tell me something really tough, like the color of my underwear."

"You're not wearing any underwear," she said, and Mitch put his feet down.

"What do you want?" He glared at her through the dusty sunlight. "If you just stopped by to screw up my day, you're done."

She looked around the office again and walked over to the coatrack with a hip-rolling step that strained the fabric of her tight skirt and lessened Mitch's annoyance considerably. Then she picked up his linen jacket, walked back to the chair he kept for clients and dusted off the seat with it. Mitch would have been annoyed again, but she bent over to dust the seat, and while the lapels on her jacket were crossed too high to make the view really breathtaking, everything sort of moved forward against the loose, soft fabric, and he remembered that he really didn't like linen that much, anyway. Then she walked back to hang up his jacket, and he watched her from the rear and thought again what amazing creatures women were and how glad he was that he was male.

Then she sat down, and he tried to pay attention.

She blinked at him, her eyes huge. "This has to be confidential."

Mitch snorted. "Of course it does. Nobody ever walks in here and says, 'Listen, I want everybody to know this.'" He pulled a yellow legal pad toward him and picked up a pen. "Let's start with your name."

"Mae Sullivan," she said, and he wrote it down.

"And what seems to be your problem?"

She glared at him. "Someone *seems* to have murdered my uncle."

Her voice was snottier than he'd imagined a really sexy voice should be. It wasn't easy being aroused and annoyed at the same time. It took a lot of energy, and he needed that energy to not think about the heat, which was another reason to dislike her. "Murder. Well, you know, the police are excellent at that sort of thing. Have you reported the body yet?"

"The memorial service is day after tomorrow."

"So this isn't exactly news to the police."

"The police aren't interested." Her brown eyes met his blue ones evenly. "Are you?"

Mitch looked into those eyes and thought about murder instead of divorce work and sighed. "Yes. I'm going to be sorry, but yes, of course I'm interested."

She shifted in her seat, all her moving parts meshing in elegant, erotic motion, and Mitch thought, *Thank God I don't have a partner, or she'd have offed him for sure.*

LYING WASN'T Mae's strong suit, but she was considerably cheered by what she saw. Blinking up at her, groggy with the heat that blanketed his office, Mitchell Peatwick didn't look as if he'd catch on if she told him she was one of the Pointer Sisters. He just lounged behind his Goodwill desk, his shaggy blond hair falling in his eyes, and smarted off to her while she snubbed him. When he wasn't talking, he was sort of endearing in a dumb-as-a-box-of-rocks kind of way, but he had an office right out of a dime-store novel, and his mind was obviously still in one. *The Maltese Falcon?* What a dreamer.

But that was good. It was going to take a dreamer to buy her story about the murder and the diary. And he wasn't completely impossible. He wore beat-up clothes of no particular style, and his hair could have used a trim, and his face had more jaw than it really needed, but he was solidly male, with that broad-shouldered, non-gold-chain-wearing, let-me-lift-that-car-for-you-lady kind of doofus sexiness that made women think that maybe they'd been too hasty with the liberation movement.

And then, of course, he opened his mouth, and all those women went looking for the nearest lamppost to hang him from. If he'd just kept his mouth shut . . .

On the other hand, she was looking for dumb.

"Tell me about your uncle," he said, and his voice was patient, and she thought she saw sympathy in his eyes, which made her feel guilty for using him. Of course, maybe it only looked like sympathy. Maybe it was a hangover.

"He was murdered." Mae leaned forward a little, just enough so that her breasts moved under her jacket. It had worked on him before, although she had to be careful not to overdo it. Sometimes men became jaded after too many minutes of shifting silk crepe. Or they got that glazed look in their eyes. She peered into his eyes. Still fairly alert. Full speed ahead. "But nobody believes me when I tell them that."

"Including the police?"

Mae tried to look defeated and vulnerable. He looked like the type who would go for defeated and vulnerable. Brigid O'Shaughnessy had done well with defeated and vulnerable. "I haven't gone to the police. They wouldn't have believed me. His doctor signed the death certificate. There's nothing the police can do."

He picked up his pen again. "What was his name?"

"Armand Lewis." Mae watched as his hand moved across the yellow pad, making slashing strokes with the pen. He had strong, broad hands, and his movements were sure, and she was well down the road to her own fantasy when she realized what was happening and put a stop to it. There was too much at stake to blow on a nice pair of hands, particularly a pair hooked to a brain lame enough to buy her story.

He looked up at her. "What did the doctor put on the death certificate?"

"Heart attack."

He wrote that down and then said, "Did your uncle have heart problems?"

"Yes."

"How old was he?"

"Seventy-six."

When he spoke again, he seemed to be choosing his words carefully. "Obviously, it has occurred to you that it is not unlikely that your uncle would die of a heart attack at seventy-six."

"Obviously." Mae smiled at him, Brigid to the teeth.

"Do you have a reason for thinking he was murdered?"

"No." Mae leaned forward a little and moistened her lips. "I just know he was. I have a sixth sense about things sometimes."

He smiled at her, the kind of smile people give to unreasonable small children and the deranged. "And this is one of those times."

"Yes."

"Okay." He went back to the pad, and Mae relaxed an iota. "Did he leave a lot of property?"

"Yes. His estate should be in the neighborhood of twenty million."

"Nice neighborhood. Who inherits?"

"I will, once the will is probated."

His head jerked up. "All of it?"

Mae nodded. "Half of his stock and all of everything else."

"Who gets the other half of his stock?"

"His brother, Claud Lewis."

"Does Claud need the stock?"

"No."

Mitch frowned. "And there are no bequests to servants, nothing to charity, no locked boxes to distant relatives?"

Mae shot him another Brigid smile to get him back on track. "Really, this isn't necessary. There are small bequests to the butler and the housekeeper, but they wouldn't have hurt my uncle."

"How small?"

"Fifty thousand each."

He met her eyes. "In my neighborhood, fifty thousand isn't small."

Patience wasn't supposed to be a bombshell's strong suit, but Mae didn't have much choice. Mitchell Peatwick was turning out to be a lot more focused than she'd thought. This was not good. "It's not enough for them to retire on. If Uncle Armand were still alive, they'd be making almost that much in salary every year, plus free room and board. They're in their sixties, and they're not going to find places like the ones they had with my uncle. His death was a disaster for them. Now, about my uncle—"

"I don't suppose there are a lot of calls for butlers these days," Mitch agreed. "Still, give me their names."

Mae took a deep breath. Why was it that men always said they wanted to help her and then refused to listen to her? Was it her, or was it some awful by-product of testosterone? "They didn't kill him."

"Give me the names."

She smiled again, a little tighter this time. "Harold Tennyson and June Peace."

"Where are they living?"

"In the house." Mae tried to unclench her teeth. The heat was making her irritable, her tight shoes were making her irritable, but mostly Mitchell Peatwick was making her irritable. "My uncle's house."

"So you're keeping them on."

"Well, of course." Mae's patience finally broke. "I can't throw them out into the snow."

He smiled at her, obviously pleased to have annoyed her. "It's July. You'd be throwing them out into the grass. And since you're not throwing them out, they didn't lose anything when he died."

Mae swallowed her irritation. "They didn't know that I wouldn't throw them out."

"They're not acquainted with you?"

"Of course they're acquainted with me. But I never promised I'd keep them on if anything happened to Uncle Armand. We never talked about it."

"How long have they known you?"

Mae smiled at him. "What difference does it make?"

"If they have known you for any length of time, they would have known what you were likely to do. How long have they known you?"

"Twenty-eight years."

His eyes widened slightly. "Since you were born?"

"No, since I was six and went to live with my uncle."

"You're thirty-four?"

"I'm thirty-four."

"You don't look thirty-four."

"That's because I'm not married." Mae's smile felt as if it were set in concrete. "Marriage tends to age a woman."

"Doesn't do much for a man, either."

"Actually, it does. Married men live longer than single men."

"It just seems longer." He leaned back in his chair and surveyed her with patent cynicism. "So, Harold and June dandled you on their knees and fed you cookies, but you think they didn't know that you'd take care of them for life if they offed your Uncle Armand."

Mae closed her eyes briefly. "They did not off my Uncle Armand."

"We'll get back to them later. Okay, besides you and Harold and June and Uncle Claud, there's nobody else in the will?"

"No."

"Did your uncle own a business?" He tapped his pen on the pad. "Was he involved in anything that somebody might have wanted to take over?"

"He was a partner with my Uncle Claud in Lewis and Lewis years ago."

"*The* Lewis and Lewis? The big conglomerate Lewis and Lewis?"

"Yes."

"Were there any other partners?"

"No. Just my Uncle Claud."

He opened his mouth again, and Mae moved to block him before he took off in another wrong direction. "He also did not kill my Uncle Armand."

"Did they get along?"

"No. My Uncle Claud disliked my Uncle Armand because he thought that he was profligate and libidinous and a disgrace to the good name of Lewis."

"Sounds like a direct quote."

"It is."

"Was it true?"

"Yes."

Mitch raised his eyebrows. "Libidinous at seventy-six?"

Mae sighed. Mitchell Peatwick might be a fool, but he was a persistent fool. "He kept a mistress. In fact, they made love the night he died. She tells everyone that whether you ask or not. Then she weeps."

He sat back in his chair. "Could we digress for a moment?"

Mae looked at him with exasperation. "Do I have a choice?"

"No. He was seventy-six years old with a heart condition and he made love with his mistress who was...what? Fifty?"

"Twenty-five. Her name is Stormy Klosterman. This is not relevant—"

"Klosterman?"

Mae gave up. "Her stage name is Stormy Weather. Of course, she was temporarily retired while she was with my uncle."

"Of course." He blinked. "That would have been how long?"

"Seven years," Mae said flatly. "He caught her umbrella when it rolled off the runway one night. It was magic."

He grinned at her. "Not a fan of Stormy's, I see."

Mae shrugged. "She's all right. At least, I don't think she killed my uncle. She didn't get a dime."

"Did she know that before he died?"

"Yes. He was very clear about that with all his women."

"There were more?"

"Well, there were before Stormy. I had a lot of aunts when I was growing up."

"You grew up with Uncle Armand?"

Mae thought briefly about reaching across the desk, grabbing him by the collar and screaming, "Could we get to the diary, please?" but that would have been counterproductive. *Humor him.* "My parents were killed in a car accident when I was six. In their wills, they had appointed my three great-uncles as executors and guardians. Uncle Armand, Uncle Claud and Uncle Gio. All three uncles wanted me, so they drew straws."

"Uncle Gio?" His voice sounded strangled.

"We were all in the lawyer's office, and they drew straws, and Uncle Armand won. Now can we get back to my Uncle Armand's death?"

"And Uncle Gio's last name would be . . . ?"

"Donatello."

"Terrific." He dropped his pen and stared at her with distaste.

Mae tried to get the conversation back on track. "I see you've heard the rumors about my Uncle Gio. Don't worry. They're not true. Now, about—"

"I've heard of the whole family. How's your cousin Carlo?"

"He's out already," Mae said. "It was a bum rap."

He sat quietly for a moment, and Mae felt his eyes size her up, and she realized for the first time that she might have made a mistake in coming to see Mitchell Peatwick. He looked as if he had the IQ of a linebacker, but there was something going on in that devious male mind. God knew what, but Mae was sure it wasn't good.

He leaned forward. "Okay, let's forget Uncle Gio for the moment. Aside from your sixth sense, which I'm sure is extremely accurate, you must have had another reason for coming here since, according to you, no one who knew him killed him. So tell me the truth. Why do you think he was murdered?"

This was it. Mae moistened her lips again. "You mustn't tell anyone this." She leaned forward a little to meet him halfway. "His diary has disappeared. I heard him talking on the phone about it the day he died, and now it's gone. The diary isn't important, but whoever has it murdered him. I'm sure of it."

SHE WAS LYING, of course. Mitch's take on humanity had deteriorated to the point where he assumed someone was lying if her lips were moving, but she was definitely lying about the diary. Either there wasn't a diary, or there was and it was important. Either possibility was irrelevant; what was important was to find out why she was lying.

And with this woman, it could be because of her sixth sense. Or her twenty million.

Twenty million.

Hell, with twenty million, she could lie to him forever as long as she paid him $2,694.

If only she hadn't mentioned her Uncle Gio.

He really had been interested in taking the case. And not just because of the money or because she had a terrific body. Well, okay, partly because of that. But mostly because it would have been great to take as his last case one that didn't involve drinking lukewarm coffee in parked cars outside cheap motels. He'd come to terms with the fact that his bet had been the result of a midlife crisis, and that it would have been a hell of a lot easier to just buy a Porsche and date a twenty-year-old, but somehow he'd wanted to have at least one real fight-against-injustice case before he quit and went back to being Mitchell Kincaid, yuppie stockbroker.

And then she dumped Gio Donatello in his lap. Shouting murder in Gio's vicinity tended to be unhealthy. He raised his eyes to hers to tell her that he didn't think he'd be interested, and she looked back at him, trusting and vulnerable. He couldn't tell whether it was real-vulnerable or fake-vulnerable, although his money was on fake-vulnerable, but as vulnerable went, it was very attractive.

"So." Mitch shifted in his chair, squirming as his shirt stuck to the sweat on his back. "Let's sum up here. You have a seventy-six-year-old man with a heart condition who makes love to his twenty-five-year-old mistress and dies. The doctor says it's a heart attack. You, the woman who inherits half of his stock and everything else he owns, say it's murder. The suspects are the housekeeper and the butler, his brother who inherits the other half of his stock, his mistress who inherits nothing and a local mob boss and his homicidal son, but in your opinion, none of them did it."

"That's it." She nodded. "I know these people. I've asked them if they know anything about Uncle Armand's death, and they've said no. They wouldn't lie to me."

Mitch shook his head at her naiveté. "Sure they would. The first rule in life is 'everybody lies.' Remember that and you'll get a lot further."

She blinked at him, her thick lashes making the movement much more of a production than it usually was on regular people. "That's awfully cynical, Mr. Peatwick."

"That's me. And cynical doesn't mean I'm not right. For example, I'll bet you fifty bucks you've lied to me already today."

Her eyes met his without blinking this time. "Of course I haven't." She widened her gaze, looking stricken. "How could you think that?"

Mitch grinned. "You're good, sweetheart. You're very, very good. But you blew it there at the end. Don't widen your eyes like that. Gives you away every time."

Her eyes narrowed. It was amazing. Even narrowed they looked good. Sort of bitchy and mean, but good. "Mr. Peatwick," she said. "Do you want this job?"

It was on the tip of his tongue to say no, thank you, I don't like your relatives, and besides, you lied to me, and you're up to no good, and the diary bit is too farfetched, and what the hell are you trying to do, anyway? and then he realized that the only way he'd ever find out what she was trying to do was if he took the case.

And it was a real Sam Spade kind of case.

And he needed the money to win the bet.

Mitch sighed. "What did your uncle say about the diary on the phone that makes you think somebody killed him?"

"He said, 'Don't worry. No one can get me without the diary.'"

Mitch felt depression settle over him. For the first time that afternoon, she was making sense. "Are you sure it wasn't gone before he died?"

"I don't think so." She gazed at him, wide-eyed and innocent, and he knew she was up to something. "He said that on the phone Monday evening, and he died later that night. He wrote in the diary every night, so he'd seen it the previous evening at the latest."

Mitch threw his pencil on the desk. "Okay. Five hundred per day plus expenses."

Her eyebrows snapped together. "That's ridiculous."

Mitch shrugged. "That's my price."

She scowled at him for a moment, and he smiled back, impervious. "All right." She opened her purse and took out a checkbook. He watched her scrawl the amount and her name across the check, her handwriting the first uncontrolled thing he'd seen about her.

Then she tore the check out and tossed it across the desk to him. Thirty-five hundred dollars. He took a deep breath and tried to look unimpressed. "This is for a week. What if I solve this in an afternoon?"

"You can give me a refund."

She didn't seem unduly interested in the possibility. The woman had no faith in him. Just as well. There was no way in hell he was giving her a refund.

He'd just won his bet.

Mitch walked around the desk and pulled his jacket from the coatrack. "Come on then, let's go see Uncle Gio."

She took a deep breath, and he watched in appreciation. "Mr. Peatwick, I just paid you to find the diary—"

"And I will do that, Miss Sullivan. I will do whatever you want. But first we will go see Gio Donatello."

"Why Uncle Gio? I told you—"

"I have to talk to all of these people," Mitch said patiently. "And if I manage to live through an afternoon of accusing a mob boss of murder, the rest of this case has got to be all downhill."

"Uncle Gio's not with the mob."

"Your cousin Carlo cut off somebody's finger. Who cares if they're with the mob? They're psychopaths."

She shifted in her chair. "They're just volatile."

"Volatile." Mitch snorted. "That's cute. Come on, let's go, but I'm warning you—you protect me from your homicidal relatives or my rate doubles."

She picked up her purse, contempt clear in her eyes. "Fine."

He watched her stand, pushing her weight up with her calves, which flexed roundly as she moved, and then he watched as she swiveled toward the door.

If she'd just keep her mouth shut . . .

She turned back to him, impatience making her face stern. "I don't have all day, Mr. Peatwick, and you're already wasting my time with this trip. Are you coming or not?"

His fantasy evaporated, and reality returned, still sucking. Mitch sighed and followed her out the door.

2

HIS CAR LOOKED like a two-toned aircraft carrier. Mae had known he wouldn't be the Volvo type, but she'd expected something from the current decade. "This is your transportation?"

"This is a classic." He patted a massive metal side panel. "There aren't many '69 Catalinas on the road anymore."

"Yes, and there's a reason for that." Mae touched the paint. "What exactly do you call this color?"

"Oxidized red. You getting in or not?"

"Certainly." Mae looked pointedly at the passenger door.

He grinned at her. "It's okay, it's not locked. Go ahead and get in."

Mae shook her head in disbelief. "A collector's dream like this one, and you don't lock it. What are you thinking of?"

"I have faith in my fellow man." He ambled around to the driver's side, so relaxed that Mae wasn't sure how he stayed upright.

"Then you're going to love my cousin Carlo." She tried to open the door but it stuck. "I think this is locked."

"Nah, just yank on it." He opened his door and slumped into his seat while Mae tugged on the door with increasing force. Finally, he reached over and popped it open from the inside.

"Thank you." Mae slid into her seat. "I've seen living rooms smaller than this."

He surveyed his domain with obnoxious pride. "Makes you wonder why they invented bucket seats, doesn't it?"

Mae bounced a little on the rock-hard seat. "No."

He turned the key in the ignition. "You snotty rich people are all alike. Can't appreciate the simple things in life."

"I am not rich." Mae gazed at the vast interior of the car. "And I wouldn't call this simple."

"You're not rich?"

"No." Mae tugged at the seat belt, trying to get it across her lap. "I had a trust fund once, but it died. When the inheritance clears, I will be rich, but until then, I just cleaned out my checking account for you." She gave up tugging and turned to him in exasperation. "Mr. Peatwick, I don't think this seat belt works."

He leaned across her to yank on the belt himself, and she breathed in the scent of soap from his hair. He yanked on the belt again, rocking slightly against her, and she stopped breathing for a moment in the sudden flush of heat she felt.

This was not good.

He yanked again, and the belt unspooled, and he leaned back into his seat and clicked it in place for her. "There. Just like one of those fancy new cars, only better."

Mae brought her mind back to where it belonged: away from Mitchell Peatwick.

He shoved the car in gear and backed out of his parking space. He pulled out into the street, and the rear of the car bounced as the wheels hit the pavement. "Where exactly does Gio live?"

Mae told him and then watched him drive, absentmindedly answering his questions about Armand and steering him back to the diary whenever he drifted too far afield. His hands were loose on the wheel, large and supple, and his fingers slid over it when he turned a corner. She'd never been a hand freak before, but then, she'd never met Mitch Peatwick before. *He's dumb,* she told herself, *and he's macho, and he's going to be another one of those let-me-take-care-of-*

everything guys who's just out for himself. There was a reason she'd given up men, and Mitchell Peatwick was a perfect example of it. She'd paid him to find the diary, but he wanted to see Gio, so of course they were going to see Gio. Whatever you want, Miss Sullivan. Right. As long as she wanted what he wanted.

She glared at him.

He stopped in the middle of one of his questions. "What? What did I say?"

"Nothing," Mae snapped. "Absolutely nothing."

MITCH LEARNED only one thing on the drive over to Gio Donatello's place: Mae Sullivan wanted that diary. He'd tried half a dozen times to bring up unhappy business partners, disgruntled ex-girlfriends, irate husbands, anyone who might possibly have a reason to give an old man a heart attack, but she dismissed his suggestions every time and returned to the diary. Stubborn beyond belief, that was Mae Sullivan. She would be pure screaming hell to live with, no matter how good she smelled or how soft she was when you were trying to put a seat belt around her in a purely professional capacity. Of course, he was stubborn, too, but that was different. You had to be stubborn if you were a private eye. Otherwise, you starved.

He wondered if her Uncle Gio was as stubborn. Probably more so if the rumors were true. Even so, he wanted to see Gio first. More important, he wanted Gio to see his open, honest, Boy Scout face so Gio wouldn't get annoyed with him and kill him. Uncle Gio was nobody to mess with.

His caution grew as they were waved through the heavy gates of the Donatello estate by a large, scowling man with a bulge under his jacket, and then ushered through the massive door of the sandstone mansion by another large, scowling man with a bulge under his jacket and finally led through cream-and-gold hallways to Gio's office by a small, scowling maid. She had no bulges anywhere, but Mitch was willing to bet she was still lethal.

The first thing he saw as he went through the door was a huge, vivid painting of the biblical Judith, darkly beautiful and triumphant, holding up the severed head of her enemy, Holofernes. He cocked his head at Mae and said, "Relative of yours?" She rolled her eyes at him and took his arm to turn him toward the massive desk in front of the wall of windows to his right.

And then he was face-to-face with Gio Donatello, diminutive and deadly, and his giant grandson, Carlo, the finger chopper.

Gio barely spared Mitch a glance. He shot out from behind the desk and swept his niece into his arms, shouting her name and calling to his grandson to back him up on how beautiful she was, how healthy she looked, how long it had been since she'd seen them—three whole days.

Meanwhile, Carlo Donatello stood like a god in the sunlight and eviscerated Mitch with his eyes.

"Uncle Gio, I want you to meet Mitchell Peatwick," Mae said, and Gio turned his little obsidian eyes on Mitch. The air in the room grew colder and heavier.

"Who's he?" Gio's voice was like a stiletto.

Mae patted her uncle's arm. "It's all right. I'm not dating him. He's a private detective I've hired."

The temperature went up a few degrees, Carlo abandoned Mitch to look at Mae with all the helpless longing of a science major for a cheerleader and Gio tightened his arm around Mae's shoulders. "Mae, baby, you don't need a P.I. when you've got us to take care of you. You want something found out? Carlo will find out for you." He turned back to Mitch. "You're fired. Leave."

Carlo moved toward him, and Mitch took a step back.

"*No*, Carlo." Mae's voice stopped her cousin in his tracks. "I hired him. I want him. I have a problem, and I want a professional."

Carlo didn't listen any better than his grandpa. "Mae, honey, I can do anything you want. You don't need this creep."

Mae smiled at her cousin and said, "No," and he stopped talking and just stared at her, his mouth slightly open, his eyes glazed with love. Mitch shook his head in sympathy. This guy had it bad, which was always a mistake. Maybe if he read *The Maltese Falcon*...

"Let us handle this, Mae," Gio said, and Mae said, "No, I want to do this myself," and Mitch wondered how many times she was going to have to say it before they gave her what she wanted.

Several times, it turned out. Mitch had stopped listening since hearing Mae repeating no had dulled his nerves, so he started when Gio barked, "Sit." He looked up to see the old man back behind his massive desk, glaring at him.

Mitch sat.

Mae sank into the chair next to him. "I hired Mr. Peatwick to investigate Uncle Armand's death."

"You hired him to check out a heart attack?" Gio's face was incredulous. "What is he, a doctor?"

"No." Mae smiled at him, and his face smoothed out, and Mitch reminded himself not to do anything to annoy Mae while he was in reach of her Donatello kin since she was obviously the center of their existence. "He's just a private detective checking out a few things for me. This is what I want, Uncle Gio. Please."

Gio nodded. "So be it." He turned to Mitch. "Ask."

Mitch double-checked, just to make sure. "This is all right with you?"

Gio shrugged. "Whatever Mae Belle wants, Mae Belle gets."

"Mabel?" Mitch turned to Mae, incredulous. "Mabel?"

"Mae. Belle." Mae made the words distinct and separate. "I do not use my middle name."

"Mabel." Mitch shook his head and turned back to find Gio glaring at him. "Oh. Great name. Really." He regrouped. "Now, Mr. Donatello, when was the last time you saw Armand Lewis?"

Gio scowled at him. "June 11, 1978. Any other questions?"

Mitch scowled back. "Yeah. What happened on June 11, 1978, that you remember the date?"

"I graduated from high school," Mae said. "I told you this was a waste of time. He hasn't seen—"

"Hey, I'm doing this," Mitch said shortly, and Carlo stirred ominously in the seat beside him. Mitch sighed. "If that's all right with you, Miss Sullivan."

"Of course." Mae sat back and waved her hand at him. "Go ahead."

Mitch turned to Gio, who glared at him. He glanced back at Carlo and saw his scowl deepen. Behind him, Judith gloated on the wall, and Holofernes was still dead. *Get out of here now,* he told himself. It was the only intelligent thing to do.

On the other hand, he had more questions, and he sure as hell didn't want to come back. He took a breath. "Did you ever have business dealings with Armand Lewis?"

"Once." Gio's face was impassive, but remembered rage bubbled beneath the surface. Mitch was willing to bet there was a reason it had only been once.

"Did you know he kept a diary?"

"No." Gio's eyes flickered at the question, but that could have been anything. The eyes of most psychos flickered at odd moments.

"Do you know of anyone who had a reason to kill him?"

"No." The flicker was back again. For some reason, Gio's temper was rising. And it had been stratospheric when they'd walked in.

The hell with this. Time to go.

He stood up, and Mae and Carlo rose on each side of him.

"I'll see you out," Carlo said, and Mitch turned to him.

"That reminds me, where were you Monday night?"

Within seconds, there was a gun in Carlo's hand, and almost as quickly, Mitch took one step back and one step to the right so that Mae was squarely between him and Carlo.

"Put that thing down," Gio barked at his grandson, but Carlo had already let his gun hand drop as soon as Mae was in range.

"Oh, this is impressive," Mae said over her shoulder to Mitch. "Aren't you supposed to be protecting me?"

"No." Mitch met Carlo's appalled eyes with a shrug. "I'm supposed to be investigating your uncle's death. Somebody pulls a gun, you're on your own."

"God, what a loser," Carlo said to Mae. "Where'd you get him?"

Mitch felt wounded. "Hey, if I wasn't almost positive that you probably wouldn't shoot her, I wouldn't be doing this." He looked down at Mae apologetically. "A man has needs, you know."

Mae blinked. "Needs?"

"Yeah. And top on my list is staying alive." Mitch eyed Carlo over her shoulder. "Could you disarm your cousin so we can go?"

"Put it away," Gio snapped, and Carlo tucked his gun away under his jacket. "Carlo's a little jumpy right now," he explained.

"Listen, if I'd killed Armand for shopping me, he wouldn't have gone peaceful in his bed," Carlo told Mitch. "Get real, bozo."

"Shopping you?" Mae echoed.

Gio watched Mitch warily. "It's nothing, Mae."

Oh, terrific. Two psychos, two motives. Mitch had never wanted out of a place more. "Well, that should about do it. Thanks for all your help. We've gotta go now."

"Good." Mae crossed to her great-uncle and hugged him goodbye, while Mitch followed, keeping an eye on Carlo.

"You take care of yourself," she scolded the old man. "I'm going to check with Nora about your blood pressure when I come back on Sunday, and it had better be down again. You hear me?"

Gio's face went to mush. "Now there, don't you worry about an old man." He patted her shoulder. "You hear that, Carlo, how she worries?"

"I hear, Grandpa." Carlo glared at Mitch. "Mae's a good girl."

"Well, let's go." Mitch edged toward the door. "Great meeting you all."

"Just a minute, honey." Gio caught at Mae's arm and nodded at his grandson, and somehow Mitch found himself alone in the cream-and-gold hall with Carlo, who immediately slammed the door behind them, grabbed a fistful of his shirt and hauled him off his heels the inch that brought them nose to nose.

MAE WINCED as the door slammed shut after them. "I have to go, Uncle Gio. Carlo's going to do something to him."

Gio's face leaned closer to hers. "What's this about, Mae Belle?"

"Nothing I can't handle." Mae patted his hand and then pried it off her arm.

"You know we'll give you anything," Gio insisted. "Anything at all. Let's get rid of the P.I."

Mae patted his hand again. He was fussy and he never listened to her, but she loved him, so she tried to erase the worried look in his eyes. "I'm fine. All I want is my private detective for a week or so. That's all." She stopped, distracted by a thud from the hallway. "Oh, hell, Carlo's beating him up." She stooped and kissed Gio's cheek with an audible, affectionate smack that made him grin, and then she headed for the doorway. "Call Carlo off, will you? I don't need him screwing things up for me."

"He'll just keep an eye out," Gio answered, but she was already through the door.

"TELL HER you quit," Carlo had growled in Mitch's face as the door closed behind them, his godlike handsomeness distorted with hate. "Right now."

"Your interpersonal skills need work." Mitch jerked Carlo's hands off his jacket and smoothed the worn cloth as his heels hit the floor again. "Of course, that was obvious when you cut off that guy's finger but—"

"She doesn't need you." Carlo shoved his face in Mitch's. "She's got me."

Mitch glared back at him. "Lucky her."

"Tell her you quit *now*," Carlo said, practically spitting the words.

"No," Mitch said, and Carlo punched him.

Mitch slammed into the wall and slid slowly down to the floor, his head ringing, hitting the carpet just as Mae came through the door.

"*Carlo!*" Mae swung her purse and caught him a good hard clip across the shoulder. "Damn it, he's my detective. You leave him alone."

"Aw, Mae." Carlo rubbed his shoulder, but he seemed a lot more upset by the force of her anger than by the force of her blow. "It was just a tap. It didn't even hurt, did it, Peatwick?"

He glared down at Mitch, who glared back and wiped the blood from his mouth. "Of course it hurt, you Neanderthal." He turned his hand over and showed them the blood. "See that? That's blood. If there's blood, there's pain. It's like smoke and fire. What the hell's wrong with you?"

Carlo reached down and grabbed his shirtfront again and hauled him to his feet. "Don't be such a wuss."

"That's enough, Carlo." Mae's voice was sharp with warning. "Let go of him."

"I'm just helping him up." Carlo released Mitch's shirtfront and patted him on the back with enough force to dislocate a lung. "He's got something to tell you, Mae. Don't you, Peatwick?"

Mitch scowled up at Carlo's glare. "Yeah." He turned to Mae. "Your cousin is a psychopath. Are you ready to go?"

Carlo moved toward him, and Mae pushed herself between them. "Don't hit him anymore, you hear me? If I want him to quit, I'll fire him. You stay away from him."

Carlo's movie-star face creased with unhappiness. "I was just trying to protect you. This guy—"

Mae put her face very close to his. "Stay. Out. Of. My. Business. Understand?"

Carlo shot Mitch a glance of pure loathing. "Whatever you want, Mae."

Mae folded her arms and held her ground. "At the moment, I want him. Back off."

To Mitch's amazement, Carlo backed up a step.

"I'll see you Sunday for dinner." Mae's voice was soothing, and Carlo relaxed visibly as he gazed at her. "Take care of Uncle Gio."

"All right." He scowled at Mitch again. "You have any trouble with this guy, you call me."

"You'll be the first to know." Mae tugged on Mitch's arm.

"Actually, *I'd* prefer to be the first to know." Mitch let himself be towed down the hall, keeping an eye on Carlo over his shoulder. "At least promise me you'll give me a head start."

"Come on." Mae didn't bother to conceal her exasperation as she pulled him through the front door to his waiting car. "I'll take you home and get you cleaned up. You're a mess."

"Thank you." Mitch dabbed at his bloody mouth. "What a wonderful client you've turned out to be."

"Don't whine," Mae said. "It's bad for your image."

MAE'S HOUSE wasn't as palatial as Gio's, but it was impressive nonetheless, a wedding cake of a mansion piped with white trellises. Mitch surveyed the facade as he got out of the car and then turned to Mae. "Doesn't anybody in your family live the simple life?"

"Uncle Claud lives in a very small condominium on River Road," Mae offered. "He's very austere."

"River Road is pretty expensive austere," Mitch said, remembering his own condo payments there.

Mae climbed the wide, shallow steps to the front door. "You said simple, not cheap."

"I meant," Mitch began, and then Mae reached the door, and it opened before she could touch it, and he got his first glimpse of the butler.

As a butler, Harold made a nice bouncer. Still, he was a slight improvement over the bulging scowlers at Gio's, looking more like a seedy aristocrat on steroids than a garden-variety thug. He nodded formally at Mae and stepped back from the door. "Good afternoon, Miss Mae."

"Good afternoon, Harold." Mae nodded to him just as formally, and walked past him into the house, and Mitch trailed after her, wondering who they thought they were kidding.

The place was impressive in its oppressive elegance. Everything was dark, rich and heavy: paneled walls with red brocade inserts, figured carpets in oriental reds and greens, massive walnut posts on the curving staircase. The overall effect was one of great weight. It wasn't the kind of place that anyone had ever dashed through, laughing gaily.

Mitch resisted the urge to ask for a flashlight and followed Mae farther into the dim hall.

Harold frowned at him as he closed the door after them. "Who's the stiff?"

Mitch turned back to him. "Excuse me?"

Mae took Harold's arm and drifted deeper into the hall, leaving Mitch to follow. "This is Mitchell Peatwick. He's the private investigator I've hired to look into Uncle Armand's death."

"So this is what you and June cooked up." Harold sounded displeased.

Mae jerked her head at Mitch. "Not in front of the help. We'll discuss it later."

"I am not the help," Mitch said with dignity. "I'm a professional."

Both Harold and Mae shot him incredulous glances, and then Harold turned back to Mae. "This is a bad idea."

"Maybe so, but it's the only one I've got, so we're going with it." Mae stopped. "I'm hungry."

"Tray in the library in ten minutes." Harold moved toward the back of the hall. "Don't spill."

Mae caught his arm to stop him, stood on tiptoe, and kissed his cheek, and Mitch's opinion of butlerhood as a career improved. "I never spill."

"Tell that to the library carpet." Harold moved on again.

"What's he mean, 'Who's the stiff?'" Mitch scowled. "Who's he calling a stiff?"

"You, evidently." Mae nodded toward the door through which Harold had just vanished. "Come on out to the kitchen. I'll get you cleaned up and then we can talk in the library."

Mitch's first impression of the kitchen was a lot of gleaming white tile and massive appliances surrounding a Marilyn Monroe look-alike.

"Oh, my." She smoothed her white dress over her hourglass figure, and Mitch realized belatedly that she was sizing him up. "Is this him?"

"This is Mitchell Peatwick, June." Mae went past her to the sink and pulled down a paper towel before she turned on the tap. "He's the private investigator I hired."

June tilted her head to survey him, her blue eyes caressing every inch of him. "Very nice."

"Thank you," Mitch said. "It's about time I got some appreciation."

"Oh, poor baby, what's wrong?" She pulled out a chair and motioned him to it, every movement sensual and pleasing, and Mitch blinked as the butter of her charm flowed over him. For some reason, she reminded him of Mae, which made no sense because there was nothing butterlike about Mae. "Is that blood on your mouth?" June asked him.

"Yes. I met Mae's cousin Carlo." Mitch sat in the chair and then jumped a little as June laid soft, gentle fingers against his face to tip it up to her.

"Poor baby," June cooed again, and Mitch stared at her, fascinated. Her oval face had the soft blurring that women got as they aged, but she was still stunning.

Harold came in from the pantry and dropped a trayful of plates on the table with a clatter, glaring at Mitch in a definitely unbutlerlike manner. "Mae's hungry," he said pointedly to June, and she smiled one last time at Mitch and went to the refrigerator.

Mitch leaned toward her automatically as she went, and then caught himself as a midsize, sloppily spotted dog of no particular breed joined them from the pantry and collapsed by the counter. Harold ignored the dog and stomped away while June began to haul out food: a leftover roast, two fat tomatoes, a slab of cheese, a plastic bag full of greens, a gallon of milk.

Suddenly, Mitch was starving.

Mae caught his attention by bringing the wet towel over from the sink, nudging the dog away with her foot to get to him. "Get away from the counter, Bob." Bob immediately returned to his place by the cabinet.

Mitch opened his mouth to ask Bob about the diary, but then Mae bent over to see his face, and he looked directly down the front of her jacket to the pink lace bra she was wearing. There was a lot of lace, and a lot more of Mae. "My God."

Mae put her hand under his chin and yanked it up. "First June and now me. Stop ogling or I'll tell Carlo."

"It'll be worth it. Ouch!"

Mae dabbed at the cut on his lip. "Don't be such a baby."

"Be careful, Mae." June looked up from the cutting board where she was slicing minislabs off the roast and dimpled at Mitch while Mae used a lot more force than he thought was necessary to clean his lip. Then June caught sight of Bob and patted her hip. "Come here, Bob. Get away from the counter."

Bob blinked at her and yawned.

Mae dabbed at Mitch's mouth again, gentler this time, and he looked up into her eyes. "Sorry about Carlo," she said softly, and pressed the towel against his lip for a moment, and Mitch forgot she'd been nasty. In fact, as far as he was concerned, she could hold that towel there forever, her face tipped close to his, her scent drifting to him, her jacket gaping open. It was the best he'd felt in a long time. A few more hours with Mae, and he might even get back his enthusiasm for life.

Then she stepped back and surveyed her handiwork, and the mood was broken. "That'll do it. You're fine. He barely tapped you."

"Thank you for the sympathy." Mitch scowled at her.

Harold came back from the pantry with a loaf of homemade bread on a breadboard and a huge knife. "Get away from that counter, you dumb dog."

A bird chirped outside, and Bob swung his head around and smacked it sharply into the cabinet.

"I told you to move," Mae said to him, but Bob just blinked at her.

"He does this a lot?" Mitch asked.

"Daily," Mae said. "He's male. Like you. He never learns."

"Be nice, Mae," June said.

"Food in the library in five minutes," Harold said. "Take Bob before he brains himself again."

THE LIBRARY was like the rest of the house, full of dark paneling and heavy furniture upholstered in rich, dark colors, this time complemented by shelves of leather-bound books in dark brown, blood red and deep green, some protected by locking glass doors, all looking as if they'd never been read.

Mitch had to fight the urge to shove the heavy velvet drapes back from the windows and let in a little light. "Nice place," he said to Mae as he sat at the massive table in the middle of the room. Bob collapsed next to him, laying his head across Mitch's shoe.

Mae looked at him as if he were demented. "You think so? It makes me want to scream. I always want to open the drapes. Now, about the diary—"

Mitch leaned back in his chair. "I like libraries. Mostly because I've dated a lot of librarians. Some of the best experiences in my life have been in libraries." He gazed around, noting for the first time that some of the brocade inserts in the paneling had dark squares where the fabric had faded around something that no longer hung there. He opened his mouth to ask Mae about it, but she interrupted him.

"About the diary," she said pointedly.

Mitch thought about insisting on following his own train of thought and then looked at the stubborn set of her mouth and gave up. "All right," he said. "Tell me about the diary."

Mae walked over to one of the glass-fronted bookcases while Mitch watched her in appreciation. If he got nothing else out of this case, at least he got to watch Mae Belle Sullivan move. She turned the key to open the door, and pulled down the last leather-bound volume from several rows of identical volumes.

"These are all Armand's diaries," she told him as she turned back to him. "There were fifty-eight of them, one for every year since he turned eighteen. He had these bound specially for him, and he kept them locked in this case. This is last year's diary." She handed it to him.

The book was thick and heavy, about five by seven inches, bound in hand-tooled leather and stamped on the spine with Lewis and the date. Mitch flipped it open to the middle and began to read Armand's account of the evening at the opera followed by a night with Stormy. Three pages later, he looked up to see Harold delivering a tray loaded with thick sandwiches, tankards of milk and chocolate-chip cookies the size of small Frisbees.

Mae surveyed him across the table. "Found a good part, did you?"

"I can't wait to meet Stormy." Mitch closed the book and dropped it on the table, startling Bob, who raised his head and smacked it on the underside of the tabletop. Mitch winced, and then turned his attention to the butler. "Harold, how long have you worked here?"

Harold straightened. "Twenty-eight years. If you need anything else, ring." He nodded toward the small brass bell on the table, but his tone implied that Mitch could ring until the millennium and still not get service.

When Harold was gone, Mitch picked up a sandwich and said to Mae, "He came when you did?"

"Yes. Uncle Gio sent him. Now, about the diary..."

Mitch listened to Mae with one ear as he bit into the sandwich. It was full of slabs of roast beef, tomato and cheese, and he felt even more kindly toward June than he had before. She was pretty, she was warm and she could make sandwiches. Men had gotten married for less. Not him, of course, but some men. He chewed and swallowed, then broke into Mae's explanation of how Armand had written daily in his diaries to ask her, "Why did Uncle Gio send Harold?"

"He didn't trust Uncle Armand." Mae peeled the bread off the top of a sandwich and picked up a piece of cheese. "Can we talk about the diary?"

"Look, Mabel. You can argue with me and waste time, or you can answer my questions. Why didn't Gio trust Armand?"

Mae put down her cheese, exasperated. "This is ridiculous. Uncle Gio did not kill Uncle Armand."

"I didn't say he did. Why didn't he trust Armand?"

Mae glared at him. "All right. Fine. This is just a guess, but I don't think Uncle Gio thought that Uncle Armand wanted me because he wanted a child of his own."

"Why?"

"Because he was never much interested in me once I got here." Mae calmed down. "I think one reason he fought for me was because he liked taking me away from Uncle Claud and Uncle Gio."

"And what else?"

Mae shrugged. "Nothing else."

"There's got to be something else. You said one reason. That implies another reason."

"Well. I have a theory, but..." Mae picked up a slice of roast beef and began to nibble on it. "I read the diary from 1967 last night. That's the year I came. I was trying to figure out how I felt about him." She frowned at Mitch. "He wasn't an easy man to like, but I did live with him for twenty-eight years at his request. But he never liked me much." She looked more puzzled than hurt. "So I read the diary to see if my suspicions were right. And I think they were. I think it was because if I left, June would have left him."

"That would upset me," Mitch said, thinking of the food. "Why didn't he just offer her more money?"

"It wasn't the money. She was unhappy. Her son, Ronnie, had just died, and she was going to leave, and then Uncle Armand brought me home, and I think she knew I'd never get any love if she left, so she stayed." Mae picked up another slice of roast beef. "So he got to beat Uncle Claud and Uncle Gio and keep June. Putting up with me must have seemed minor in comparison."

Mitch scowled at her. Armand Lewis must have been a world-class jerk. Just looking at Mae, Mitch could tell she'd been a great kid, and now twenty-eight years later, all she could say was, "He didn't like me much." Hell of a way to treat a kid. He felt himself growing angry, and put a lid on it. She was a grown-up now and obviously capable of looking after herself, and he had a strict rule about getting emotionally involved with his clients. Of course, with his other clients, that hadn't been a problem. His other clients hadn't been Mae Belle Sullivan.

Mitch jerked his mind away from the thought. "That doesn't explain why Harold came to stay."

Mae peeled another layer off her sandwich. "Uncle Gio sent Harold because he knew Uncle Armand didn't like kids. And say what you will about Uncle Gio, he loves kids. He was worried about me. He still worries about me. So he sent Harold."

Good for Gio, Mitch thought and then stopped himself. He did not approve of Gio Donatello. Period. Back to Harold. "And Armand let Harold stay?"

Mae nodded. "I think he liked having him here for free, since Gio was paying at first. And then Harold and June fell in love, which was great because I ended up with two parents just like normal kids. So he's still here. Could we talk about the diary now?"

"That doesn't explain why Armand didn't want you to move out once you were grown," Mitch pointed out. "Maybe he really did care about you and just—" He stopped because Mae was shaking her head.

"The minute I moved out, June and Harold would have been gone." She picked up another slice of cheese. "He just didn't want to lose good help. And I couldn't afford to support June and Harold. They would have had to find a place that needed both a butler and a cook and that would give them the freedom they're used to, and it wasn't going to happen. Even at Uncle Gio's, they would just have been part of the staff. They needed a home."

"And you're responsible for giving them one?"

"Of course." Mae blinked at him, surprise apparent on her face. "They raised me. They count on me. They need me. I *owe* them."

"Oh." Mitch picked up his second sandwich. "This still doesn't make sense. Why couldn't they just stay and work for Armand?"

"Because they both hated him." Mae narrowed her eyes at him. "Do not get distracted by that. They didn't hate him enough to kill him. If they'd wanted to kill him, they'd have done it years ago." She drank a slug of milk and licked her milk mustache off, distracting Mitch from his questions. She reached for a cookie. "Now, about the diary—"

"You can't have a cookie until you've finished your sandwich, Mabel." Mitch moved the cookie plate out of her reach.

"I can have anything I want." Mae pulled the plate back toward her, but Mitch held on, and she yanked on it, knocking the rest of her sandwich onto the floor where Bob swallowed it whole and then choked for thirty seconds. Mae patted the dog on the back until he stopped hacking, and he collapsed in gratitude at her feet.

Mitch shook his head in contempt. "Is he okay?"

"Yes." Mae smiled affectionately at the dog. "He's dumb, but he's okay." She turned back to Mitch. "Go ahead, inhale your next sandwich. I can do the Heimlich."

Mitch picked up his sandwich. "So why do you want the diary?"

"Because whoever has the diary killed my Uncle Armand," Mae said piously as she reached for a cookie. "I think justice should be served."

"Because you loved him so much."

"Actually, I didn't even like him much, but that's beside the point. The point is—"

"That you want the diary. I know, I know." Mitch put the rest of his sandwich back on his plate. "The memorial service is the day after tomorrow?"

Mae nodded as she chewed her cookie.

"And Gio and Carlo and Claud will be there."

Mae nodded again.

"Who else? Stormy?"

Mae nodded and swallowed the last of her cookie. "And also most of the business community, like Dalton Briggs. He's been hanging around a lot lately, and he was engaged in some sort of business deal with Uncle Armand. And I suppose some of Uncle Armand's ex-girlfriends might . . . oh, God." She froze with her hand over the cookie plate. "Barbara."

"Barbara?"

"Barbara Ross. She's been dating Uncle Armand. Very high-society stuff." Mae looked ill. "She's going to meet Stormy. Oh, poor Stormy, first Armand dies and now this. This is going to be awful. I'm going to have to think of something."

Mitch frowned at her distress and then at himself for caring. He pointed at the most recent journal. "It says here that Armand set Stormy up in a town house."

"He kept a place a few miles from here. She used to live there, but I'm pretty sure she moved out."

"Do you have a key?"

"To the town house?" Mae nodded. "Harold has one. He went over and brought a box of Uncle Armand's personal stuff home. The rest of his clothes are in boxes for Goodwill. They're still there, so we still have the key."

"Okay. I'll pick you up at nine tomorrow morning. I want to see the place. I also want to look around this house and talk to Barbara Ross and Stormy, but I want to see the town house first."

Mae looked exasperated. "The diary's not there. Harold looked."

"Forget the diary for a minute. There are other things of interest in that apartment." Mitch stood up. "In the meantime, can I take a couple of the old diaries with me?"

Mae scowled up at him. "But what I want is—"

"I know. The one that's missing," Mitch finished. "Let me do this my way."

"Do I have a choice?"

"No."

Mitch went to the bookshelves, and Mae rang the bell. Harold appeared.

"What?" he said. "The game's on. I'm missing it."

"Wrap up the rest of this stuff for Mr. Peatwick, please." Mae waved her hand at the food on the tray. "He has a lot of heavy reading to do tonight, and he'll need food."

Mitch turned back from the bookcase with three volumes in his hands. "You're a good woman, Mabel. Spoiled rotten, but basically good."

Harold snorted and stalked out with the tray, closely followed by Bob, and Mae rose to look at the diaries he'd taken.

"Okay, 1967 I get. That's the year I came. Why 1977 and 1978?"

"I want to know what Armand did that made Gio so mad he never talked to him again." Mitch picked up the 1993 volume from the table and added it to the stack in his arms. "I may be back for more."

"Why?" Mae didn't even bother to hide her annoyance. "That's all in the past. I want—"

Mitch put his free hand over her mouth and was momentarily distracted by the softness of her lips against his palm. He was getting distracted a lot today. Must be age. *Concentrate*, he told himself. "Look, you want to find your uncle's killer. And the only way to do that is to find out what made your uncle killable. You do want to find his killer, right?"

Mae's eyes met his, huge and wary, and she nodded as he took his hand away. "Right."

You're lying to me again, Mabel, Mitch thought, but all he said was, "Well, then, that's what we'll do. As soon as I've read these diaries, we'll go find who killed him."

3

WHEN MITCH WAS GONE with the diaries and a care package of food, Mae leaned back in her chair and considered her situation. Mitch was definitely going to annoy everybody in Riverbend, but he'd probably been doing that for years. Still, if she could keep him focused on the diaries, he could easily drive whoever had the missing volume to give it up and probably to take to drink, too. And keeping him focused might be easier now that he actually had some of the diaries in his hands....

That made her think about his hands. Bad move. Of all the times for her hormones to kick in, this was the worst, but there it was. Ever since she'd met him, she'd had that bubbly feeling under her skin that she hadn't felt for a good long time. It was a nice feeling to have, but not in conjunction with Mitchell Peatwick. He was arrogant and stubborn and his face looked like a catcher's mitt with a jaw. And she absolutely was not going to get herself mixed up with a man who didn't listen to her; she had enough men not listening to her in her life already.

Absolutely not.

Sure she was once again in control of the situation, Mae wandered back to the kitchen and sat down to pry the heels she'd borrowed from June off her feet.

"Thank you," she said, handing them back. "They were agony."

"Poor baby." June put the shoes on the counter. "Do you want a basin of Epsom salts?"

"No." Mae rubbed one of her reddened feet. "I want the money so we can move to a better place than this mausoleum and live like normal human beings and you won't ever have to worry about the future again. This is driving me crazy."

"I cleaned Armand's room today," June said. "The painting of that nude woman is gone."

Mae stopped rubbing. "The Lempicka? How long has it been gone?"

"I don't know." June sank into the chair at the end of the table. "I think it was there last Wednesday when I did the room, but I'm not sure. I hate that damn room."

"I know. Don't worry about it. Pretty soon we'll get the inheritance and move and you won't ever have to see this place again." Mae took June's hand and held it tightly until the older woman smiled and relaxed again. Then Mae went back to the current problem. "He might have sold the painting."

"I don't like it." June's pleasantly vacuous face turned grim. "He never let anything he owned go, and then suddenly everything starts disappearing. There's something really wrong here."

Mae nodded. "Whatever it is, it'll be in the diary. He said, 'They can't get the money without the diary' that day on the phone. We need that diary."

"Well, maybe your detective will find it for us. He seems quite nice." June's voice softened. "If it wasn't for Harold, I'd be quite interested."

Mae grinned at her lovingly. "I think he feels the same. He was looking at you with a lot of appreciation."

June flapped her hand. "Oh, he was just detecting." She leaned back in her chair. "What did you think of him?"

"Well, I thought he was dumb as a rock." Mae tried to sound disinterested. "But I'm not so sure. I think he's just different."

"Different how?" June prompted.

Mae shrugged. "Oh, he doesn't act macho or protective or charming or any of the usual garbage. He just asks me questions and looks down my jacket and treats me like...anybody." She rubbed her foot again. "He's really up-front about being a loser."

June studied Mae under her eyelashes. "I don't think he's a loser. And I don't think he thinks you're just anybody. He seemed quite interested in you."

"He just likes women." Mae sat back. "And the more I think about it, the more I don't think he's as dumb as I thought he was."

"I don't think he's dumb at all." June smiled. "I think he's going to be good. Maybe we should tell him the truth and let him take care of everything."

"No." Mae's voice was firm. "Letting men take care of everything means you end up with nothing. Besides, you should have seen him at Uncle Gio's. Carlo pulled a gun, and he stepped behind me."

"Smart man." June nodded approvingly. "And so attractive."

"Oh, please."

"I'm serious." June leaned forward. "Your problem is that you've always been with those pretty boys. Carlo and that worthless Dalton. Now, Mitchell Peatwick isn't pretty, but he's..." She stopped, obviously searching for the right word.

"Earthy?" Mae suggested.

"All man," June said, and Mae groaned. "Listen to me, sweetie, I know men. And I will bet you that Mitchell Peatwick could give you a very good time in bed."

Mae closed her eyes to shut out the thought, but her mind flashed to Mitch's hands moving across the notepad, to his body solid on hers as he'd yanked on the seat belt, to his grin kicking up her pulse as he'd quizzed her in the library. Then she thought about him in bed and immediately squelched the feeling the thought stirred. That way lay madness. "He'd probably forget I was there." Mae shoved back her chair and stood up, unbuttoning the waistband of June's pink skirt. "Oh, God," she sighed as the zipper unzipped itself down her hip. "That feels so good."

June smiled up at her. "So would Mitchell Peatwick."

"Not in a million years," Mae said.

"We'll see," June said.

THE MIDSUMMER HEAT filled Mitch's dingy apartment like fog. He stretched out on his battered iron bed in his white boxer shorts, trying not to dissolve in his own sweat while he read Armand's 1978 journal. Armand's style wasn't exciting, but his plot line was riveting. Having already finished reading the 1967 and 1977 diaries, Mitch knew that finding somebody with a motive for killing Armand was not going to be a problem. Finding eight pallbearers would be a stretch, but locating people with a yen to kill Armand Lewis would be a piece of cake.

Somebody knocked on his door. Since his entire apartment was one room and a bath, Mitch didn't have to move. "Come in," he called and looked up to see his best friend and sometimes partner close the apartment door behind him.

Neatly pressed and stern with disapproval, Newton was the epitome of a stockbroker who had just caught his best customer buying lottery tickets. His pale blond eyebrows rose up his well-bred forehead, a forehead already so high it seemed limitless, and his pale blue eyes glared behind his gold-rimmed glasses. "You know, it is not a good idea to live in this neighborhood with your door unlocked. Extremely impractical. Foolhardy. There's no reason for this. The bet didn't say you had to live in penury."

"I'm supporting myself with the profits of the agency, Newton. That was the deal." Mitch glanced around the room before he grinned at his friend. "It's not so bad. I actually like it better than my old River Road place. It's got more character." He stopped for a moment, thoughtful. "You know, I'm glad I sold that condo. At least that's one part of my old life I won't have to go back to."

Newton's nostrils flared as he took in the stained wallpaper and cracked floor tile. "This is abysmal." He turned his survey on Mitch. "I see you finally did your laundry."

"I had to." Mitch went back to the diary. "Somebody noticed I was going without underwear. There's food on the table."

"You bought authentic food?" His friend's voice was incredulous, and Mitch looked up, annoyed. Newton was staring in amazement at the remains of June's care package on Mitch's rickety table. "Truly astounding." He bent his attenuated frame closer to the table, his beautifully cut suit refusing to crease even as he moved. "These are cookies."

"Yes."

Newton's patrician nose quivered like an upper-class rabbit's. "Homemade?"

"Yes. There's milk in the fridge. Oh, and there's this." Mitch dropped the diary on the bed and rolled over to pick up his pants from the floor and pull his wallet from the back pocket.

Newton took a plastic bottle of milk from the refrigerator. "You didn't buy milk in this. Who's giving you food?"

"The same woman who gave me this." Mitch handed over Mae's check.

"My God." Newton sank into the kitchen chair, milk in one hand, check in the other. "You did it. You won the bet." A smile spread over Newton's prim lips. "Our friend Montgomery is not going to be pleased."

"Then he shouldn't have made the bet." Mitch smiled back as vast satisfaction spread through him. "You know what part I like best? I did it all by starting completely over as Mitch Peatwick. I made it without using Mitchell Kincaid's credit or connections. Montgomery is going to hate that part. That's the part of the bet he thought was going to sink me."

Newton's smile widened. "I'll mention it when I call him tonight."

"Why the rush? You didn't by any chance make a side bet?"

"A substantial one." Newton's smile widened. "He implied that I never took risks, and I let him manipulate the stakes."

"I'm touched." Mitch's voice was light, but he really was moved. "How much did you risk on me?"

"Twenty thousand."

Mitch's smile vanished. "Forget touched. I'm stunned. How the hell did you ever bring yourself to risk that much?"

Newton blinked at him. "It wasn't a risk. I was betting on you."

Mitch closed his eyes. "Never bet that much on me again. What if I'd just given up?"

Newton shook his head as he put the milk bottle down and pocketed the check. "I'll deposit this in the account. And as for giving up, that would never happen." He stood and crossed to the cupboard and took out a Flintstones glass, looking at it dubiously before he rinsed it out in the sink and went back to the table to pour the milk.

"Well, at least tell me next time." Mitch leaned his head against the iron bedstead. "That way I'll know what's riding on my impulses."

For a moment, Newton seemed to lose himself in judicious reverie. "No," he decided. "I don't want to affect your thought processes."

"Newton, most of the time I don't have thought processes."

"I know." Newton gazed at him with respect. "I admire that."

Mitch gave up. "At any rate, the game's over. I made the detective agency solvent in a year and supported myself with the profits, you've got your money back, and I've soaked Montgomery for ten thousand. Now we can all go back to real life." Mitch's glance fell on the diary. "As soon as I've figured out this last case."

Newton stopped, his cookie halfway to his mouth. "You're quitting the agency?"

Mitch nodded, understanding. "I know. I'm not all that excited about turning back into a yuppie stockbroker myself, but I've got to tell you, Newton, being a private detective sucks. You'd hate the people."

Newton's face fell. "No Brigid O'Shaughnessy?"

"Well, almost." Mitch called back the image of Mae walking into his office. "You should meet Mabel."

"Mabel?" Newton bit into his cookie. "Sounds like a barmaid." Then the taste of the cookie registered on him. "These are excellent. Really epicurean." He chewed methodically and endlessly, evidently savoring the bouquet of the cookie as if it were a fine wine.

"June made them. She's Mabel's housekeeper and cook."

"Tell me all." Newton took another bite.

"A very attractive woman with fantasy breasts came into the office today and hired me to find her seventy-six-year-old uncle's killer. After that, things went downhill."

Newton chewed his bite of cookie for the thirtieth time and swallowed. "Murder? That seems farfetched. Who's the uncle?"

"Armand Lewis. It seemed farfetched to me, too, at first, but now I don't know. He kept diaries, Newton, and there's some very interesting stuff in them."

"Armand Lewis." Newton frowned. "He has a very shaky reputation."

"Had. He's dead. What do you mean, shaky?"

"People had a tendency to lose money in his vicinity. Do you really think he was murdered?"

"I'm open-minded on that." Mitch picked up the diary. "I'm only on the third one of these, but there are a hell of a lot of people who are not going to be weeping at the memorial service on Friday."

"Such as?"

"Well, June the cookie-maker, for one. She had a fifteen-year-old son named Ronnie who got into drugs back in 1967. Summer-of-love stuff. She asked Armand for help sending him to a detox place, and Armand said no. Four months later, Ronnie OD'd."

Newton frowned. "It was ungenerous of him, but hardly a motive for murder."

"The kid was Armand's son."

Newton blinked.

"June gave her notice as soon as Ronnie was buried." Mitch handed Newton the diary marked 1967. "It's all in there. He just says that he's glad Ronnie's off his back, but he's worried because the only reason June stayed was so that the boy would be with his father. Then she gives notice, and he says flat out that the reason he wants his orphaned niece to come live with him is because he thinks it will keep June."

"Orphaned niece?"

"Our client." Mitch smiled and then realized he was smiling and stopped. "Mae Belle Sullivan. She was six in 1967 when June's son died. Armand took Mae to give June another kid to raise so she wouldn't leave."

"Do you think June killed him?"

Mitch shrugged. "Could be. But we also have Harold Tennyson, the butler. He came at the same time Mae did to keep an eye on her, and immediately fell hard for June who is still quite a looker. Back then, she must have been a knockout." He stopped, distracted. "Mabel is not a knockout. She is merely very attractive, which is why she has little or no effect on me."

Newton blinked at him. "What?"

"Nothing. Anyway, Harold's smitten-ness amused Armand, so he tried to get June back again to spite Harold, even though they hadn't been any more than employer and employee since he'd found out she was pregnant years before. Only June wasn't playing." Mitch grinned. "Armand sounds truly annoyed in the diary. It's toward the back. You should read it. I enjoyed it immensely. Anyway, Armand pushed his luck one night, and Harold roughed him up a little. Armand fired him, but June threatened to quit, and little Mae cried, and the guy who sent Harold in the first place leaned on Armand, so Armand had to take him back. And they've hated each other ever since. There are a couple of places in the diary where Armand says he thinks Harold is trying to kill him. Accidentally backing the car over him, stuff like that."

Newton frowned. "Is Harold homicidal?"

"Harold is a longtime employee of Gio Donatello."

Newton blinked. "Dear Lord."

"Gio is another of Mabel's uncles. He also doesn't like Armand, partly because of Mae, but also because—" Mitch picked up the 1978 diary and handed it to Newton "—Armand bilked him out of a quarter of a million in 1978."

Newton's face took on the stern disapproval of his Puritan ancestors. "That was stupid."

"That was Armand." Mitch shook his head. "He's also cheating on his girlfriend with a society woman, both of whom may be feeling less than warm toward him. And then there are any of his business partners who he may have screwed, including his brother Claud. I haven't read the most recent journal yet. I can only imagine the carnage this jerk may have caused lately."

Newton raised his eyebrows. "His brother is Claud Lewis?"

"Yep."

"I think I might be more afraid of Claud Lewis than I would be of Gio Donatello." Newton chose his words carefully, as always. "Gio can only kill you, and there's no real evidence that he's ever murdered anyone. But Claud can ruin you financially, and there's ample evidence that he's done that whenever the spirit moved him."

Mitch thought for a moment. "Can you look into Armand's financial dealings? Especially his dealings with Claud?"

"I can ask around." Newton looked uncomfortable. "It's really none of my business."

Mitch rolled his eyes. "Newton, you're the one who's always saying you want to be a detective, too. If you're a private detective, it's your business to look into things that are none of your business."

"Oh."

"You said you wanted to help with the agency. This is the first time I've had something that involved skills beyond peeping and waiting. This is the good stuff, Newton."

"All right." Newton seemed to gather himself up. "All right. I'll do it."

"It's for a good cause," Mitch comforted him. "I think Armand Lewis died a natural death, but if he didn't, he didn't deserve to be murdered." He cast a doubtful glance at the last diary. "Probably."

"Probably?"

Mitch frowned. "What we have here is a man who has annoyed or hurt everyone he's ever known, and he's known a lot of powerful people. And the beauty of it is, he's written it all down in his diaries. Of course, he thinks it's a scream that he swindled Gio and perfectly understandable that he deserted his own son, but even so—" Mitch picked up the most recent diary "—he wrote it all down in these. Just like Nixon and his tapes. Ego makes people stupid, Newton."

"In that case, the last diary should tell you who killed him," Newton said. "If anybody did."

"That's what's interesting. The last diary is missing."

"Oh."

"Yeah." Mitch propped the 1993 diary on his knees. "If it wasn't for that, I'd say Mabel had lost her grip. But the thing about Mabel is, she may be unreasonably stubborn, but she's not stupid. And she's up to something." Mitch met Newton's eyes. "She's lying to me, Newton. Can you believe it?"

"Just like Brigid," Newton said.

"That's what I'm afraid of," Mitch said.

WHEN MITCH WENT DOWN to the street to get his car the next morning, all four tires were flat, every one slashed through the rubber. He called the service station, his insurance agent and the police, and then he called Mae. Even over the phone, her voice went right to his spine. *Forget it*, he told his spine. Then she said, "Hello?" again, and he said, "Someone appears to have stabbed my tires."

"Mr. Peatwick?"

"Call me Mitch, Mabel. It's friendlier. You're going to have to come pick me up."

"All four tires?"

"Yes. I have a sixth sense about these things, and I'm willing to bet you any amount of money that your psycho cousin Carlo killed my tires. I don't think he was listening when you told him to leave me alone."

He heard a sigh on the other end of the line and told his spine to ignore that, too. "I'll pay for the tires," she said.

"Thank you, that won't be necessary. Vandalism is covered by insurance. Now come and get me." He gave her directions and then waited while she wrote them down.

"Uh, Mr. Peatwick?"

"Mitch."

"This is in Overlook."

"Yes, I know."

"Oh. Dangerous neighborhood."

"Actually, it was a nice little place until your cousin dropped by. He lowered the tone considerably."

"I'll be right there."

"Thank you," Mitch said, but she'd already hung up, and he felt curiously bereft for a moment. *This is just a case*, he told himself. *She is just a client*. Yeah, right, his spine said.

HE WAS OUT in front of his tenement sweating in the morning sun when Mae pulled up in her brown Mercedes. He seemed bigger and bulkier than she'd remembered. The same stubborn lock of blond hair fell in his eyes, and he leaned against the grimy building in the nastiest part of town with no indication that he recognized the tawdriness around him. He got in the front seat, held his hand gratefully in front of the air-conditioning vent, and said, "Great car." Mae said, "I hate it," and he said, "Why?" and she pulled away from the curb.

From the corner of her eye, she could see him looking her over from the passenger seat before he closed his eyes and turned away. "You look very nice today," he told her while he stared out the windshield.

Mae glanced down at her flowered black sundress. "Thank you." The dress was a big change from June's pink power suit, but it was a lot more the real Mae than spike heels and veiled hats. She felt an irrational glow of pleasure that he liked real Mae clothes on her, and then she kicked herself mentally. It didn't make any difference what Mitchell Peatwick liked. Back to business.

"I'm truly sorry about your tires," she began.

"It's not a problem." He made himself comfortable in the leather seat. "I've alerted the neighborhood-watch association, and they'll keep an eye out from now on."

They drove past a parked car just as a spindly teenager put a crowbar through the window and grabbed the radio.

"Should I stop?" Mae asked, checking the rearview mirror as she slowed.

"Why? You've already got a radio."

Mae tried to rein in her exasperation. "I thought you might like to make a citizen's arrest."

Mitch snorted.

"Well, you're a private detective. I assumed—"

"Don't," Mitch advised her. "Assuming is always bad. I, for example, assumed that since you were driving an expensive luxury car that you'd like it. Why don't you?" He blinked at her, looking more like a doofus than ever, but Mae wasn't fooled.

Not anymore.

"Why don't you like this car?" he persisted, and Mae sighed.

He wasn't going to quit asking. The thing about Mitch wasn't that he asked such brilliant questions. It was that he asked dumb questions and asked them and asked them and asked them and *asked them*, and eventually you told him everything you knew just to make him shut up and go away. Well, maybe not go away. . .

"If you didn't like this car, why did you buy it?"

Mae gave up. "I didn't. I bought a beautiful little blue Miata which was more than I could afford, but I loved it so much, it was worth the sacrifice."

"More than you can afford?"

"I told you, I'm not rich. My uncles are rich. I make fifteen thousand a year as the volunteer coordinator for the River-bend Art Institute."

"You *work?*" Mitch sounded incredulous. "How come you're not working now?"

"Because my uncle just died, and the memorial service is tomorrow." Mae turned out of Overlook and onto the wide boulevard next to the university. "I have to go back to work on Monday."

"Oh." Mitch was silent, evidently digesting new information, and then he asked, "So how did you end up in a car you hate?"

Mae began to smile in spite of herself. "You are incredibly persistent."

"One of my finest qualities. Why did you buy this—"

"I didn't. My Uncle Armand did. He didn't like the Miata, and it was sitting in his garage, and only the best could sit in his garage, so he traded it in for this chocolate shoe box."

Mitch frowned. "That's illegal. The title wasn't in his name."

Mae rolled her eyes in scorn. "If you think that would stop my uncle, you haven't been reading his diaries."

"As a matter of fact, I have. Well, at least you got a great car for free."

"No, I didn't." Mae turned down a tree-lined street of old brick German town houses. "He paid the difference between the Miata and this car. I still have to pay off the amount of the Miata loan, which was more than I could afford in the first place. So now I'm paying it on a car I don't even like, thanks to my Uncle Armand, may he rest in peace." Mae pulled up in front of the last town house on the right. "This is it."

"Maybe he did it for you," Mitch suggested. "Maybe it's safer—"

"He did it for him," Mae said flatly. "My Uncle Armand didn't exist without his labels. Anything near him had to be expensive. Anything else caused him real pain. It bothered him that I was driving a car that wasn't high-class enough, so he changed it so he wouldn't be bothered anymore. Then he expected me to be grateful. I wasn't. That, in a nutshell, is the story of our relationship. Any other questions?"

"Can I drive this car on the way back?"

"Pay attention," Mae said. "You're investigating a murder."

"I know that," Mitch said. "I just want to investigate it driving a Mercedes."

Mae gave up and got out of the car, leaving Mitch to follow her.

HAROLD'S KEY got them in the front door. Mae led Mitch into the cool, narrow hall as she cast a quick glance up the stairway.

"What's up there?" he asked.

"I don't know. I've never been here before." She moved to the end of the hall and through an archway into the living room, and then stopped, overwhelmed by envy.

The room was small but cozy, full of soft amber upholstered furniture and pretty crocheted pillows and flower prints, everything washed with the sunlight that came through the French doors at the end of the room. Mae walked to the doors and leaned against the doorjamb, looking out into the tiny walled garden that still bloomed with the last of the summer flowers. Everything was so pretty, so warm. She bit her lip and wondered what it would be like to live in a light-filled place with somebody who listened to her and laughed with her and put his arms around her and told her that he loved her. It was never going to happen to her, but she did wonder.

For a moment, she felt so sorry for herself, she almost cried.

Mitch moved to stand behind her, looking out over her shoulder, and she felt vaguely comforted by his nearness. "When the will is probated, we're going to move to a place on the river," she said to him. "It's going to have big open windows and clean hardwood floors and white gauze curtains, and when the breeze blows in off the river, it will fill the whole house."

"Sounds nice." Mitch's voice was hesitant, and she knew he didn't have the slightest idea what she was talking about, but at least he sounded sympathetic. And he was listening.

She turned to him. "And we're going to have about twelve dogs."

"So much for the clean hardwood floors."

She met his eyes. "It's what I've always wanted. I hate all that velvet and brocade and money at Armand's. All the furniture is too valuable to sit on, and all the books are too valuable to read, and we can't let the sun in because it will fade all the damn velvet." She stopped, aware that her voice was rising. "All we want is a home, June and Harold and I. And that's what this place makes me think of. A home." She gazed at all the comfort in the sunny little room. "Armand wouldn't know how to make a room this nice. Stormy must have chosen this stuff."

A small voice startled them. "I did."

Mitch started and turned around, and Mae saw past him to the childlike woman standing just inside the archway to the room.

She'd forgotten just how amazingly beautiful Stormy was. Her red-gold ringlets and huge blue eyes were dazzling, but mostly it was Stormy's skin, opallike in its translucence that took people's breath away. At twenty-five, Stormy Klosterman was the closest thing to perfect beauty Mae had ever seen.

Mae shot a glance at Mitch and sighed. He had that stunned look that men usually got when they saw Stormy. It wasn't his fault. Even women tended to stare openmouthed at Stormy. But it still hurt, which was dumb because she didn't care who Mitch stared at.

"I'm sorry." Mae moved past Mitch to meet the young woman. "We didn't know you were here, or we'd never have barged in on you. Are you all right?"

Stormy sniffed. There were beautiful bluish shadows under her eyes, and her mouth turned down at the corners. "Yes. It's all right that you're here. I don't live here anymore. Nobody lives here anymore." Her face crumpled and she began to cry, and Mae put her arms around her and led her to the couch.

"I'm sorry, honey." She looked back over her shoulder at Mitch, who was evidently frozen by the combination of beauty and tears. "Get her a drink of water, will you?"

"Sure." Mitch blundered past them, trying a closet door before he found the door to the kitchen, only to return with a glass of water. He looked at Stormy with no enthusiasm whatsoever.

"Go away," Mae told him.

"Right," he said, and she heard him climbing the stairs a moment later.

"I'm sorry," Stormy said when she was all cried out. She straightened her head from Mae's shoulder, and Mae watched with envy as all the pinkness from her crying jag faded into rose-blushed cheeks.

"Have you been alone all this time?"

"Yes." Stormy sniffed. "I've been mostly at my new place, but I come by everyday, just to say goodbye." Her face crumpled again.

Mae patted her on the back as Stormy's head hit her shoulder again. "I'm sorry, Stormy. I should have called you. I just didn't think."

"That's okay." Stormy's voice was muffled in Mae's shoulder.

"Is there anything I can do to help?"

Stormy pulled back a little and looked at her wistfully. "Maybe we could have lunch sometime. Like we were friends, sort of."

"Lunch?" Mae nodded, a little confused but grateful to have found something that cheered her up. "Sure. This weekend, maybe?" Friday was the memorial. There was no way she was taking Stormy to lunch before the memorial.

"Saturday." Stormy beamed at her, and Mae blinked again at how beautiful she was and how volatile. In anyone else, the mood change would have been a sign of mental instability. In Stormy, it was childlike and enchanting. And Armand had planned to leave her to go to Barbara Ross? "I'd like that," Stormy finished. "Lunch. Saturday would be good. At the Levee. I like the Levee."

"Oh, me, too." Mae did a quick calculation to see if she had enough money to cover lunch at the Levee. Paying Mitch had tapped her out. Maybe if she sold the Mercedes.

"Why are you here?"

Mae started, but Stormy's voice was still friendly. "Uh, I . . ." Telling Stormy that she'd hired a detective to find Armand's murderer was probably not going to be a good move at this point. "I'm looking for something."

"Who's the guy?"

Mae blinked at her again.

"The guy you came with. He's cute." Stormy wrinkled her nose in pixie appreciation.

"Cute?" Mae stared at her. "Mitch?"

Stormy nodded. "Like a teddy bear. Is he yours?"

"Uh, no. I hired him."

"For what?"

Mae spoke slowly, taken aback by Stormy's sudden focus. "To find Armand's diary. We thought it might be here."

Mitch's voice broke in from the doorway. "Well, it isn't."

Stormy turned to him and smiled. "I know. All his things are packed up. Harold came and took some of them."

"The diary isn't in the box that Harold brought home," Mae told her. "Is there someplace here he might have hidden it?"

Stormy shook her head, her ringlets dancing in the sunlight. "No. There's no place like that here." She held out her hand to Mitch. "I'm Stormy."

He came forward and took it. "Hi, I'm Mitch. Can you think of anybody who might have wanted to kill Armand?"

"Kill him?" Stormy's voice sounded stunned, and Mae mentally kicked Mitch around Greater Riverbend. "He died of a heart attack. I was there. We were making love and he died. *In my arms.*" She started to cry again on the last words, and then she collapsed back onto Mae's shoulder.

Mae glared up at Mitch, but he just stood there, staring at Stormy with a frown on his face.

"I loved him." Stormy sobbed. "Nobody believed that. They all thought it was for the money. But I loved him."

Mae patted her again. "I believe you."

Stormy stopped crying and sat up, blinking at her. "You do?" She sniffed. "I always liked you."

"Oh. Thank you." Mae stood up before things got any weirder or, worse, before Stormy started to cry again. "If you're all right, we really have to be going." Mae backed away from her and bumped into Mitch. "We'll see you at the memorial tomorrow."

"Oh, will Mitch be there, too?" Stormy stood and drifted after them.

Mitch took Mae's elbow. "Wouldn't miss it." He pulled her through the archway, and Mae waved once to Stormy and then went gratefully, eager to be gone from all the beauty and loneliness and strangeness in the town house.

4

MAE WAS SO DEEP in thought that she handed over the keys to Mitch without argument when he asked for them.

"What's wrong with you?" he asked her when they were in the car.

"Stormy."

"No kidding." Mitch put the key in the ignition. "That woman is strange. What's her IQ, twelve?"

"I think she was upset," Mae said nobly, trying to defend Stormy without feeling cheered that Mitch wasn't impressed with her.

"That whole setup is strange," Mitch went on. "Why would he buy her another place when they had that one?"

Mae frowned in agreement. "That's not the only thing that's strange. Could you explain to me why a man would cheat on a mistress as beautiful as Stormy?"

"Sure. That's easy." Mitch started the car and pulled out onto the road. "He's a guy."

Mae felt the anger that she'd been nursing for Armand's insensitivity veer toward Mitch. "There are a lot of men who don't cheat on their lovers."

"No, there aren't."

Mae glared at him. "Is this based on personal or professional experience?"

Mitch looked over at her condescendingly. "Don't get huffy because you don't like the facts. I'll admit I see a lot of it because I get hired to look for it, but the fact is, men cheat. We have to. It's a biological imperative."

"An imperative," Mae repeated. "This would be testosterone we're talking about here, right?"

"Well, that's part of it. But a lot of it is just man's need to see what's beyond the next hill. It's the reason men crossed the oceans, built the pipeline, opened the West." Mitch waved his hand, obviously feeling expansive. Iron Mitch.

"So you're saying my Uncle Armand cheated on Stormy because he couldn't open the West?"

Mae put an edge on her voice, and Mitch looked over at her warily. "I don't suppose we could let this drop."

Mae set her jaw. "No, I don't suppose so."

"I don't know why women always get so upset over this." Mitch shook his head, clearly mystified. "This is just the way men are. It isn't in our nature to commit."

"And why is that?" Mae asked between clenched teeth.

Mitch turned onto the street that led into Mae's high-rent district. "All right, let's say I'm married." He shot a stern warning glance at Mae. "Of course, I'm never going to get married because I don't believe in it and there are still a lot of librarians out there that I haven't kissed, but for the sake of argument, let's say I'm married."

Mae settled into her seat, her jaw still clenched. "This should be good."

"And let's say my wife is beautiful, intelligent, exciting, with terrific legs and the world's most perfect breasts. I mean, perfect breasts. High. Round. Smooth." He took one hand off the wheel and cupped it in the air. "Firm. The kind that bounce but don't shimmy, if you know what I mean."

Mae raised her eyebrows. "Been thinking about this a lot, have you?"

"No. I never think about women's breasts. Where was I?"

"Bounce, no shimmy."

"Right. So I'm married to the perfect woman with perfect breasts, but then I see another woman. On a street corner, maybe."

Mae frowned at a woman in a blue dress on the corner. She was leaning into the wind, unnecessarily, in Mae's opinion, and the dress molded itself around her curves. "On a street corner."

"Right. And she has a nice figure, nothing like my wife's, of course, and her legs aren't as good, and she's just attractive not beautiful."

"And the point is?"

Mitch shrugged. "I want to see her breasts."

"Why?" Mae said. "I thought you just said your wife—"

"Yes, but I've seen those. I want to see these."

"Even though they're not as good."

"Well, yeah, but they're still good."

Mae thought for a moment. "Suppose she turns out to be a *Playboy* centerfold. If you buy the magazine, will that do it?"

"No."

"Suppose she's a stripper, and you get to see them for real. Will that do it?"

"No."

"But you're seeing them," Mae said, exasperated.

"I'm seeing them, but all I did was pay money to see them from a distance. I need to personally—"

"Open the West." Mae glared at him. "You are disgusting."

"No, I'm not," Mitch protested. "I'm not married, and I never will be, and I have never promised a woman I wouldn't see other women. I am free to open the West anytime I want."

"You're still disgusting."

"Look, there's no point in getting upset about this. You can't understand because you're a woman, and women don't think like that."

"Women don't want to open the West?"

"No. Women want to stay home and keep the East looking nice."

Mae took a deep breath as a red mist rose before her eyes. "You're deliberately trying to make me kill you, aren't you?"

"No." Mitch's voice was the Voice of Reason. "This is just biology. Men need multiple breasts in their lives. Women need to make a commitment to one penis."

"That is garbage," Mae said flatly.

"Then why do women always want to get married? Because they want to commit to a penis."

"Then why do men get married?"

"For backup. That way, they always have a set of breasts at home."

Mae picked up her purse, using every ounce of self-control to keep herself from hitting him with it. "Stop the car, I'm getting out."

Mitch blinked at her in alarm. "Why?"

"There's a man on the corner back there, and I think his penis is bigger than yours."

Mitch scowled at her. "Don't take this out on me. This isn't about me. We're talking about *other* guys here. I'm not married. I don't cheat. And anyway, you've never seen my penis, so how do you know his was bigger?"

"Well, I can't be sure, of course. But I want to *find out*. I feel this need to *explore*, to *lay pipeline*, to *open the West*." Mae craned her head to look behind her. "Turn around. I'm pretty sure we can find him."

"You don't want to open the West," Mitch dismissed her. "You just think you do because of women's liberation."

"Long." Mae lingered on the word. "Thick. Hard. Throbbing. Bobs not droops. I can see it now. Take me back. I want him."

"You are no lady." Mitch turned down the road to Mae's house. "Besides, a good detective never gets distracted on the job. We're working. Pay attention."

"Whoa." Mae turned her head to watch a man on a motorcycle go past. "Look at that one. Hello, Daddy, come to Mama." Mitch pulled into the driveway, and she opened her car door before he was completely stopped. "If anybody asks, tell them I went West."

"Very funny." Mitch caught the skirt of her dress as she got out and yanked her back into her seat against him, and she tried to ignore the heat his hand generated against the small of her back. It was such a little thing, but it made her throat close and her breath come shallow, and when she turned to look at him, he was staring at her with a funny look on his face. He pulled his hand away and cleared his throat and said, "Are you going to help me find out what happened to your uncle or not?"

"I suppose so. Duty calls." Then she remembered what they'd been arguing about. "And after all, there'll be another man along any minute. And it's okay because *I'm not married.*" She beamed at him and slid out of the car before he could catch her this time.

"This is not an attractive side of you," Mitch called after her. She ignored him, but she heard him sigh, and then he followed her into the house.

June wasn't home, so they foraged for food on their own.

Mitch stared at the mounds of food inside the refrigerator: plastic-wrapped trays of cold cuts and vegetables, tiny chilled petits fours, gallon jugs of punch. Bob joined him, and they surveyed the feast with equally wistful eyes. "You have enough food here for an army."

Mae came to stand beside him, distracting him from the food.

She was distracting him a lot lately.

"That's all for the memorial tomorrow." Mae pushed past him to rummage on a lower shelf. "How do you feel about leftover lasagna?"

"Enthusiastic." Mitch told himself not to watch her as she bent over farther to get the lasagna, but he did, anyway. He was human. And so was she, thank God.

He wondered how long it would take for her to get over her snit about opening the West. Probably days.

She pulled the lasagna from the fridge and nudged the door shut with her hip as he backed out of the way. Then he watched as she put the lasagna on the counter and stretched to take down two plates from the cabinet, nudging Bob away from the counter with her foot. Her dress was loose, but it pulled against the muscles in her arms and back and flowed over her rump, and he sighed just from looking at her.

He'd never met a more watchable woman in his life.

That was odd, when he thought about it. He'd known a lot of very attractive women, many of them more attractive than Mae Belle Sullivan. All right, not many, but some. Stormy Klosterman, for one. So why was he watching her more and more and thinking about the case less and less and Stormy not at all? This was a bad sign in more ways than one.

A smart man would tell her he was investigating the rest of the case on his own.

Mae slid lasagna-filled plates into the microwave, tapped in the time, punched the power button and turned back to him. "So where are we going this afternoon?"

Mitch said the first thing that came to mind. "I want to meet Barbara Ross, the woman who convinced Armand to leave Stormy."

"I thought he did that because he had to open the West."

"Well, sometimes you get a trail guide to take you, so to speak."

Mae laughed and Mitch grinned back.

"Does this mean I'm forgiven?"

"For what? That drivel in the car?" Mae shook her head. "Well, you're a macho jerk, of course, but at least you're an honest macho jerk. You didn't try to convince me that you had to go West for my own good, or that deep down inside, women *want* men to go West. You're up front about being a jerk. That's kind of nice."

"I object to the jerk, but if it gets me off the hook, I'll take it."

"It gets you off the hook." The microwave dinged, and Mae turned to pull the lasagna out.

Good. Now she was happy again, and he could leave her at home and get to work.

"And you're not fooling me with this sudden need to see Barbara," she added. "You just want to meet more women." She put the lasagna on the table and distracted him by smiling at him.

Suddenly, leaving her behind held no appeal. "With you there as a chaperon? Hardly. What else are we having besides lasagna?"

"Bread." Mae went into the pantry to get it, and Mitch watched her move.

Okay, so he'd tell her tomorrow he was working alone. After the memorial service.

A bird chirped outside, and Bob swung his head into the cabinet with a resounding thunk.

"I know just how you feel," Mitch told him and went to see what Mae was doing in the pantry.

BARBARA LIVED in an elite condo about four blocks from Armand's house.

Mitch swung the Mercedes into a parking space. "Birds of a feather."

Mae got out and stared up at the building, wilting in the heat. "I'd rather die than live here."

"Fortunately, you don't have to make that choice." Mitch came up behind her. She didn't move, so he put his hand on the small of her back to push her toward the door, enjoying the warm dampness there. When he realized how much he was enjoying it, he jerked his hand away. "No one will ever make you live in an overpriced condo."

"Somebody tried to once." Mae walked toward the door.

"Who?"

"My ex-husband."

Mitch stopped. "You were married?"

Mae looked back over her shoulder. "It didn't last long. Four years."

Mitch scowled, annoyed for some reason. "Four years is long. You lived with some guy for four years?"

"Four years is not long for a marriage. Marriage is supposed to be forever. And no, he didn't open the West, if that's your next question." Mae pushed through the lobby doors.

"I wasn't going to ask." Mitch followed her into the air-conditioned opulence, upset, wondering why he was upset. So she'd been married. Big deal. It was none of his business. "So what happened?"

"It didn't work out."

"Because you didn't like living in a condo?" What kind of a fool had this guy been? If she wanted to live in a tent, Mitch would have . . . He stopped himself. No, he wouldn't have. He was never getting married. But if he did get married, and it was to someone like Mae, he'd live in a tent if that was what it took to keep her. "You left because you didn't like the living arrangements?"

Mae rang for the elevator. "I didn't leave. He did."

"What a fool," Mitch said, and Mae smiled at him.

"Thank you. That's very sweet of you."

Mitch shrugged. "Just an observation. Nothing personal."

The elevator stopped, and Mae put her hand on his arm. "There's just one thing I want you to know."

Mitch tried to look understanding and supportive. "Yes?"

"If Barbara cries, it's your turn to pat."

"No way in hell," Mitch said and held the elevator doors open so she could pass through.

The maid was dark, thin and irritated at being bothered. Obviously, this was a job for someone with charm, so Mitch stood back to let Mae operate.

"We've come to see Ms. Ross." Mae smiled at her. "Please tell her Mae Sullivan is here."

"She's not here. She's still in Barbados. She'll be back tomorrow."

The maid started to close the door, and Mitch stuck his foot in it. So much for charm. "When tomorrow?"

The maid glared down at his foot. "In the morning."

Mae met Mitch's eyes. "Maybe she doesn't know about Armand." She turned back to the maid. "Do you know if she's planning on attending the memorial service for Armand Lewis tomorrow?"

"Of course she's planning on going." The maid stared at Mae as if she thought Mae was insane. "She's the widow, isn't she?"

"She is?" Mae's mouth dropped open. "The widow? Are you sure?"

"Sure I'm sure." The maid moved her head from Mae to Mitch. "Now, if you don't mind, I have things to do."

Mitch moved his foot, and she slammed the door in his face.

"She's the widow? They're married?" Mae slumped against the wall. "He married her?"

Mitch put his hands in his pockets and watched her deal with the blow. "When would he have had time to marry her?"

"Last week, I guess. He was out of town all last week, but he came back on Friday to be with Stormy, and he spent Saturday and Sunday at the house with us. He was on the phone most of the time, but he was with us. And he went from us to Stormy on Monday night, and then he died."

"And he never mentioned getting married. That is something he would have mentioned, right?"

"Well, you'd think so." Mae swallowed. "It must have been that week he was gone." She looked up at Mitch. "If he did get married, what would that do to the will?"

"I don't know." Mitch frowned. "It might invalidate it. She'd get something under Ohio law."

Mae pushed herself away from the wall and turned back to the elevator. "Come on."

Mitch trailed after her. "Where are we going now?"

"Uncle Claud," Mae called back. "If it's about money, Uncle Claud has the answer."

CLAUD LEWIS'S NEAT white frame condo on River Road was not ostentatious. It didn't have to be. It was sitting on the most expensive real estate in Riverbend.

"Hello, Prescott," Mae said to the graying mini-aristocrat who opened the door. "I'm here to see my uncle. I know I didn't call, but this is urgent."

"Very good, Miss Mae Belle." Prescott opened the door wider and nodded as they went past. "I'll tell him you've called to see him."

"Who does he remind me of?" Mitch asked Mae when he'd left the hallway.

"Harold. Prescott gave him a few pointers a while back when Harold decided he wanted to be a real butler. The only difference is, Prescott is always like this. Harold fades in and out."

"You can't make a silk butler out of a leg-breaker."

"Mr. Claud will see you now," Prescott said, appearing silently in the doorway.

Mae shot Mitch a look. "Behave."

CLAUD'S WELCOME to Mae wasn't as effusive as Gio's had been. He simply stood behind his desk and nodded to her and said, "Hello, my dear" with all the warmth of a carp.

He looked a lot like a carp, too: hatchet-faced, beady-eyed, lipless and remote. Mae bent over the desk to kiss him, and he inclined his head to offer his cheek without smiling. Mae's dress smoothed over her rear end as she bent, and Mitch was distracted, and when he raised his eyes from her derriere, he met Claud's.

They looked like dry ice. Unamused dry ice.

"This is Mitchell Peatwick, a private investigator," Mae said, and Claud stared at him, expressionless.

Mitch suddenly had a vision of Mae as a small child, facing Gio, Armand and this carp in a lawyer's office after losing her parents. Gio and Armand were no prizes, but Claud . . . the poor kid.

"Mr. Peatwick," Claud said flatly and sat down, staring at him.

Mitch knew exactly what Newton had been talking about the night before. Given a choice between facing down Gio or Claud, he'd pick Gio every time.

"We've just come from Barbara Ross's apartment." Mae sat down in the chair next to the desk, and Mitch followed her, watching Claud watch his every move. He felt like a rabbit being stalked by a snake. "She wasn't there, but her maid was," Mae went on. "The maid said she's Armand's widow."

Claud's eyes panned slowly to Mae. "She's mistaken."

"I don't think so." Mae took a deep breath. "It would be such a dumb lie. What if he married her? What would it mean?"

"She would inherit half." Claud evidently saw consequences only in monetary terms.

Mitch joined the conversation even though he knew it would bother Claud. *Especially* since he knew it would bother Claud. "Including half of your half of his stock," he pointed out.

Claud panned back to Mitch, his dislike palpable even though his face remained a mask. "There is no stock."

Mitch leaned back in his chair. "Why not?"

Claud's fish eyes didn't move. "Why are you here?"

Mitch was annoyed. Claud's one-note performance was getting on his nerves, and he hated being annoyed alone, so he smiled inanely at Claud to bring him along for the ride. "Mabel hired me to find Armand's killer. You wouldn't know anything about that, would you?"

Claud's eyes chilled him. "There is no killer. Armand died of heart failure."

"Everybody dies of heart failure," Mitch said. "We'd just like to know what caused his heart to fail."

Mae kicked Mitch on the ankle. "Behave," she said under her breath. "Barbara is not the only problem," she said, returning to Claud. "Things have been disappearing from the house."

Claud blinked slowly. "Things?"

Mitch frowned at her. "What things?"

"Paintings. Furniture. His coin collection is gone. The Florentine chess set. The Lempicka."

Mitch leaned toward her, exasperated. "You might have mentioned this sooner."

Mae waved him back. "It wasn't relevant. Nobody stole them. Armand knew they were gone and didn't say a word."

"Perhaps Armand tired of them and sold them." Claud's voice was like dry ice, too, creeping across the floor of the room.

Mae sat back. "Well, he took them, anyway. I don't know that he sold them."

"If he didn't sell them, where are they?" Mitch asked.

"He is unnecessary," Claud said to Mae.

Mae blinked. "Mitch? Mitch is necessary. He just has no manners. Do you know anything about the stuff that's missing?"

"I will take care of this." Claud stood up.

"No," Mae said, still sitting. "I can take care of it. I just need information. If Barbara is his widow and is inheriting half, I need to know where the missing things went. There's a lot of money at stake here. Do you know what happened—"

"You have no need to worry. I will take care of this." Claud had all the animation of a dummy at Walt Disney World, and he was equally immovable.

Mitch watched the emotions flit across Mae's face until she gave up and stood, too. "I can take care of it, Uncle Claud. I just need to know—"

"I will look into this." Claud walked to the door.

"Wait a minute," Mitch said and they turned to look at him. "Why isn't there any stock?"

Claud's eyes panned to Mae. "He is highly unnecessary."

"No," Mae said politely. "I want him."

"So where's the stock?" Mitch asked.

Claud's eyelids fluttered, but he answered, "I bought it."

"You bought it?" Mae echoed. "All of it? It was worth millions."

"Six million," Claud corrected. "It had fallen in value."

There was no expression on his face, but somehow Mitch picked up a sense that Claud was feeling gleeful about that stock buy. Six million must have been a bargain.

"Why did Armand want to sell his stock?" Mitch asked.

A fleeting emotion crossed Claud's face and it wasn't pretty. Mitch almost took a step back, but he held his ground.

Mae swallowed. "He must have been selling everything." She looked at Claud, shaken. "What was going on? What was wrong?"

Claud's face was closed again. "Nothing, my dear. He had a minor cash-flow problem, and he solved it." Claud's voice was patronizing but not cold. In fact, it was almost comforting for a carp. "Don't worry about this matter, Mae. I will take care of it."

Mae sighed. "If you find out anything, please let me know what's going on. I'm worried." She leaned over and kissed him lightly on the cheek again. "I'll see you tomorrow afternoon at the memorial."

Claud patted her arm once, and Mae went through the door, but Claud closed it behind her before Mitch could leave with her.

"Hey!" Mae called through the door.

Claud ignored her. "Now, Mr. Peatwick," he said, and Mitch sat back down, interested. What was Claud going to do? Threaten to give his credit rating concrete overshoes and throw it in the Ohio?

"You wanted to see me?" Mitch tried a man-to-man smile.

"Not particularly." Claud returned to his desk chair and surveyed Mitch over the gleaming mahogany expanse with no enthusiasm. "My niece is a very lovely girl."

So that was it. Claud wasn't anxious to have Peatwick in the bloodline. Mae's relatives were going above and beyond the call of duty in protecting her from him, a point that was moot since he wasn't interested, really, but it was annoying, all the same. He smiled at Claud blankly, trying to look as thick and obnoxious as possible, prepared to give him a really bad time in revenge. "Lovely is hardly the word for her. She's got a world-class ass. Every time she bends over, I forget my name."

Claud closed his eyes briefly. Then he opened the leather folder in front of him. "Since we're both men of the world, I'll make this brief."

Mitch looked around. "Well, two different worlds, of course. I bet they never cut off the electricity here."

"No." Claud was writing now, and when he was done, he tore off a slip of paper and handed it across the desk to Mitch who leaned forward and took it without rising.

"Ten thousand?" Mitch raised his eyebrows. "Hey, really, Mabel already paid me. Nice checks, though." He looked at the slip of paper again. "You know, Claud, you should get those ones with the monogram. These are kind of plain. Now, a monogram, that says class." He tossed the check back on the desk and flashed his best used-car-salesman smile. "Just a tip. One businessman to another."

"Very amusing. How much do you want?"

Claud still looked like a fish, but his carp was metamorphosing into barracuda. Not seeing any future in annoying him further, Mitch got down to business.

"How much do I want to leave a honey like Mabel high and dry? I assume that's the drift here? Dump the investigation?"

Claud nodded once. "That, certainly, and, of course, you will never see my niece again."

Mitch let the corners of his mouth droop. "You know, I've dated women whose families didn't like me before, but you people really hate me. And I'm trying so hard."

"How much?" Claud's lips barely moved.

Mitch shrugged. "A hundred thousand."

"Amusing," Claud said. "Twenty."

Mitch shook his head. "Twenty is chump change, Claud. A hundred."

"Twenty thousand is more than you make in a year."

"Well, that depends on the year...." Mitch settled down for a long financial discussion, but Claud cut him off.

"Twenty-five."

"Claud." Mitch shook his head. "You're not in a bargaining position here. A hundred thou or I go back to work for Mabel. Take or leave it. But act fast. She's waiting on the other side of that door, and while I admire her both physically and spiritually, she does have a temper."

Claud's face changed then, filled with such loathing that Mitch was taken aback for a moment. Then Claud picked up his pen and began to write.

"That's five zeros," Mitch said, and sure enough, when Claud pushed the check across to him, it had five zeros.

"Get out." Claud's nostrils flared, but otherwise his face was as impassive and cold as before.

"Pleasure doing business." Mitch stood and tucked the check in his coat pocket.

When he opened the door, Prescott was waiting in the hall.

"Seen Mabel lately?" he asked him, and the man replied, "Miss Mae is waiting in the car, sir," but the tone added, "you worthless creep."

"Hell of a lot of undercurrent in this place," Mitch said to no one in particular and strolled down the steps to the car where Mae sat in rigid fury in the driver's seat.

"Drive," he said as he got in, but she was scattering gravel across the sidewalk before he got the door shut.

"You know, some men find a temper really sexy, but I'm not one of them," Mitch said mildly. "So if this is for me . . ."

"Shut up." Mae peeled out onto the boulevard, stopping only when she came to a funeral home parking lot. She pulled in and parked, her abrupt stop bouncing Mitch off the dashboard, and only then did she turn to glare at him.

"Nice place." Mitch squinted through the window at the Victorian facade. "This one of Gio's parlors?"

"He bought you off, didn't he?" Mae demanded.

"Yeah." Mitch fished the check out of his breast pocket. "He did." He handed it over to her. "Generous guy, your Uncle Claud."

Mae took the check from him, scowling, but when she read the amount, she blinked. "Well, at least you didn't come cheap. Dalton got five hundred thousand, but he had to divorce me. All you have to do is walk away."

Mitch gaped at her. "You're kidding."

Mae met Mitch's eyes coolly, but he could see the misery there. "No, I'm not kidding."

"Claud bought off your husband?"

"We were pretty much not married by the time Uncle Claud paid him to leave." Mae swallowed as she looked at the check with Mitch's name on it.

"Well, I'm not like him." Mitch took the check back and pocketed it. "I think marriage is sacred, which is why I never do it."

Mae seemed to be having trouble breathing. "You're scum."

"Now here's a question for you," Mitch said as if she hadn't spoken. "Why would your Uncle Claud give me one hundred thousand dollars to dump you and your problems?"

Mae looked at him with naked contempt. "Because he knew you were corrupt and without honor."

"No." Mitch slid down into his seat and stared out the window in deep thought. "If that were the only motivation he needed, he'd be in Washington greasing senators. There's got to be a beauty of a reason behind this. I mean, I know he's protecting you, but a hundred grand is a lot to pay to protect a woman's virtue, especially since I have grave suspicions that you don't have any."

"I do where you're concerned." Mae put her forehead on the steering wheel. "Could you at least recommend another private eye?"

"You're not listening." Mitch rolled his head on the back of the seat until he could see her. "Stop pouting and think. Would your Uncle Claud, who looks like he has the first dime he ever made, pay one hundred thousand dollars to keep me out of your bed?"

"Dream on." Mae raised her head from the wheel and glared at him. "You're never getting into . . ." She stopped. "Oh." Her glare faded. "No. He wouldn't. If that's what he was worried about, he'd probably give Uncle Gio a call and just have your legs broken. Or something."

"That's not funny." Mitch winced. "Don't even kid about that."

"What did he say you had to do for the money?"

"Drop the case and stay away from you. But the part about you was an afterthought. I was really obnoxious about you, and it annoyed him, but that wasn't what was bothering him."

Mae perked up. "How obnoxious?"

"I mentioned your butt. He shuddered, but Gio would have had my liver."

"Uncle Claud wouldn't want your liver," Mae pointed out. "Your credit may be in jeopardy, however."

"My credit is comatose, anyway." Mitch frowned. "So why is Uncle Claud willing to pay a broken-down, incompetent private investigator a small fortune to stop him from investigating a murder that never happened?"

"Of course it happened."

"Not according to Claud. Would he pay that much to keep you out of jail?" Mitch watched her as she turned to him, incredulous. "If he thought you'd bumped off the old guy?"

"Are you accusing me of murdering my uncle and then hiring you to catch me?" Mae laughed at him. "Isn't there some kind of test you have to take to be a P.I.? Some kind of minimum IQ?"

"I'm saying that Claud doesn't want this investigated." Mitch frowned as he thought about it. "And he doesn't want it investigated a lot. And I think that's interesting."

"But not interesting enough to keep on investigating." Mae's glare was back in place. "You sold me out."

"Well, not yet I haven't. I'm pretty sure it's not contractual until I cash the check."

"Not a gentleman's agreement?" Mae's sarcasm was thick and acid.

"You need at least one gentleman for that. The butler was in the hall. It was just me and Claud, underestimating each other. We're both probably going to regret that."

Mae was so quiet that Mitch finally glanced over at her. "What?"

"Tear up the check."

"Are you nuts?" Mitch put his hand over his coat pocket in case she tried to lunge for it. "A hundred thousand may be spare change to you, but this is a fortune to me."

"But if you're working for me, you're not going to cash it, anyway." Mae leaned toward him, her eyes huge and plaintive. As she leaned closer, the neckline of her dress gaped open, and Mitch saw lush curves and creamy flesh and temporarily lost his train of thought. "Tear it up, and I'll believe in you again." Her voice flowed over him, low and warm, and Mitch reluctantly tore his eyes away from her cleavage and scowled at her.

"Don't believe in me, dummy. I'm a guy. Now, could we get moving? I've got to go home and call a guy I know to look into that missing stuff you just dropped on me in there." He gazed at her sternly. "You were supposed to tell me everything, Mabel. Keeping secrets from me is bad."

"It wasn't relevant," Mae began, and Mitch overrode her.

"Of course it's relevant. Tell me about it. You said a coin collection, furniture, and a lem-something."

He watched her face as she thought in rapid succession about killing him, bullying him, and then, finally, telling him what he wanted, and he grinned. She was stubborn, but she wasn't dumb. It was going to be easier to tell him the story than to argue with him, and she knew it.

Fast learner, his Mabel.

Mae sighed. "The Lempicka is a painting of this horrible nude blond woman. She's sort of mechanical and shiny-looking. Actually, she looks a lot like Barbara Ross."

"Is that why Armand bought it?"

"No, he bought it a long time ago. I was just a kid. He brought it home and showed it to me, and I said I thought it was really ugly, and he said that was because I had no taste. He told me it was a Tamara Lempicka, and he'd paid twenty thousand dollars for it." Mae shook her head. "I was disgusted. That much money for an ugly painting."

"So now twenty thousand dollars' worth of painting is missing?"

"No. Lempickas are hot right now. Barbra Streisand sold one last year for 1.8 million."

Mitch's eyes widened. "Dollars?"

"Yep. Of course, part of that was probably because it was Streisand's Lempicka, but we are definitely talking high six figures as a minimum. We're missing a small fortune. And that's just one of the things that's gone. We're missing his coin collection, Revere silver, two Whistler drawings, an Early American sideboard—"

"And you didn't ask Armand where this stuff was going?"

"He moved it out so quietly that it didn't register at first." Mae frowned at the traffic. "And then when we did notice, there wasn't much we could do. It was his stuff."

"And you don't have any idea what he did with it?" Mitch persisted, watching her face.

She turned and looked at him with weighty patience. "It was all in the last two or three months, which means that all the answers will be in the diary. Now can we talk about the diary?"

Mitch grinned at her in admiration of her latest finesse. You could sidetrack her for a while, but sooner or later, she'd get what she wanted. "You are something else, Mabel."

She grinned back at him, and he forgot his place in the conversation. "Don't you forget it," she said. "What are you going to do next?"

"Next?" Mitch blinked and came back to earth. "Oh. You're going to drop me off at my garage so I can tell the people there to put a hurry-up on my new wheels. You drive like a woman, and it scares me."

"Wimp."

"Then, tomorrow, we'll do the memorial, and then we'll start looking for the diary."

Mae watched him, suspicion blatant in her eyes. "So you're still investigating?"

"Until you do something to annoy me." Mitch sat up in his seat again. "Then I'm cashing Claud's check. So, from now on, I want some respect from you. Could we get going now?"

"You want my respect, earn it." Mae put the car in gear and when they were out on the road again, she asked him casually, "So what did you say about my butt?"

"To Claud?" Mitch shrugged, trying not to let his thoughts dwell on her rear end, or any part of her, for that matter. "I told him it was adequate."

"You lied," Mae said. "It's magnificent and you know it."

"Everybody lies," Mitch said.

MITCH CALLED NEWTON as soon as Mae dropped him off at the garage. "I need you to check on a few things for me."

"I'm still checking on the other few things." Newton sounded harried. "I'm still a stockbroker, you know. I'm still covering all your clients for you. I'm—"

"There's a beautiful woman involved here," Mitch said soothingly.

"I know, you told me. Mabel."

"Not Mabel. Mabel is not beautiful." Mitch tried not to think about Mae's big dark eyes and curving mouth. "Not technically. This woman is technically beautiful. Perfect. You should see her, Newton."

"Why?" Newton's suspicion was palpable, even over the phone.

"Because every man should see her. It'll restore your faith in humanity. Her name is Stormy Klosterman, and she was Armand's mistress. Supposedly he bought her a condo. Find out if he did."

Newton's sigh was part exasperation, part resignation. "How?"

"Seduce her."

"Me?"

"She's a redhead, Newton."

There was a long silence. "Just like Brigid."

"Better than Brigid."

"All right," Newton said finally. "In the meantime, what are you going to be doing? Seducing Mabel?"

Mitch swallowed. "No. Seducing Mabel would be hazardous to my health. And my sanity."

"You're seeing a lot of her."

Mitch remembered Mae leaning toward him and the lush curves he'd seen when she had, and his breath started to go. *Don't even think about it*, he told himself. "You don't understand. She's surrounded by homicidal men who watch her like hawks. Plus, this woman is so stubborn, she makes mules look indecisive. If her relatives didn't get me, she'd drive me crazy in a week."

Of course, it would be one hell of a week. His mind went back to those curves, and his hands sliding up to cup those curves and then down to . . . no. He loosened his tie and shoved Mae out of his mind to return to the problem of Armand, making his voice brisk as an antidote to the thoughts that were making him choke. "I'm reading the most recent diary again tonight. Armand Lewis was evidently offloading some of his capital in the form of paintings and furniture and stock, and I want to see if I missed any mention of him having a garage sale. Oh, and here's something else interesting—a woman named Barbara Ross says she's married to Armand Lewis."

"She inherits half, then. Wives get half automatically."

"Another good reason not to get married."

"Her name is really Stormy?"

"Find out. You're the detective."

"And in the meantime, you'll be doing what?"

"I'll be at Armand's memorial." Mitch sighed as he thought about it. "Watching all the people who are glad he's dead."

5

WHEN HAROLD ANSWERED the door at two the next afternoon, Mitch was in his best suit and his Frank Lloyd Wright tie.

"That is the ugliest tie I've ever seen," Harold said.

"Nice to see you, too." Mitch pushed past him and peered down the dim hall. "Where's Mabel?"

Harold closed the door. "They're all in the dining room. Don't pig out on the canapés."

"Thank you, Harold." Mitch nodded at him dismissively. "That will do. You may go now."

Harold snorted, and then the doorbell rang, and he returned to his duties.

Mitch ambled down the hallway picking up muted voices as he neared the second door past the library.

The place wasn't packed, but it was nicely filled with people who milled around sedately and chatted, obviously not overcome with grief for the departed. Mitch took a glass of nonalcoholic punch from a tray that went by and drifted to the wall where he leaned on the edge of a sideboard and watched the people mingle. Then he saw Mae across the room and stopped with his drink halfway to his mouth.

She was dressed in a short black dress that fastened with a row of tiny black buttons that curved all the way up the front to a collarless V neck. She looked round and healthy and fresh, and he gazed at her for a minute for the sheer pleasure of having his eyes on her. There was absolutely no trace of the pink-suited Brigid who'd been snotty all over his office two days before, and for the first time, Mitch wondered where she'd gotten the pink suit and high-rise heels that were definitely not Mabel couture.

Then June swayed into the room carrying a tray of canapés, dressed in a pink suit and heels, and Mitch knew. She spotted him and rumbaed over, dazzling everyone in her path.

"Mitch, darling." She jabbed the tray at him. "Have a canapé. I'll make you some real food later."

"Deep in mourning, I see." He snagged a sliver of bread decorated with a shrimp and moved the tray away from his solar plexus with his drink hand. "That's a nice suit you're wearing. How the hell did Mabel ever get into it?" He crunched down on the shrimp.

"We used a shoehorn." June poked him with the tray again. "Take a couple more. I've got to keep circulating, and these people are like locusts. I had a pin on this suit, and I swear somebody ate it."

"Why did you use a shoehorn?" Mitch picked up another bread finger. "What was wrong with the dress she's got on now?"

"This one's sexier. We were trying to seduce you into working for us." June picked up another canapé and handed it to him, forcing him to eat the one he had in order to free his hand for the new one. "Try one of these. They're Harold's favorite."

"Why were you trying to seduce me?" Mitch mumbled around his mouthful of canapé. "The money was plenty."

"We wanted you to believe that Armand was murdered." June surveyed the crowd and sighed. "I should just throw the tray in the middle of the floor and let them fight for it. Feeding frenzy."

Mitch swallowed his canapé. "June, would you please tell me what's going on?"

"I have no idea." June moved back into the crowd, which closed around her like sharks around a tourist.

"Kincaid, don't tell me you were Armand's broker." Mitch turned to see Nick Jamieson, his Kennedyesque lawyer, regarding him with horror. Tess, Nick's redheaded hellion of a wife, waved at Mitch from behind him.

"No, and today I'm Mitch Peatwick, so just go away, both of you." Mitch glanced around to see if anyone had noticed them together. "The last thing I need is a hotshot society lawyer blowing my cover. What are you doing here, anyway?"

"I worked for Armand once," Nick said gloomily. "It wasn't my finest moment but—"

"But we heard June was cooking, so we came, anyway," Tess finished for him. "Hello, Mitch, darling." She slipped her arm around Mitch and kissed him on the cheek. "What a lovely party. It's always so much nicer when the body isn't actually present, don't you think? I understand he donated it to science. I overheard one of the mourners saying it was the first thing he'd ever given away."

"Shut up, Tess," Nick said amiably.

"I don't have to behave. It's just Mitch." Tess batted her eyes at him. "Mitch likes me unpolished, don't you, love?"

Mitch smiled down at her. "I'm crazy about you unpolished. And I still can't believe you actually married this stuffed shirt. It's like Tinker Bell marrying Donald Trump. When are you going to leave him and come live in sin with me?"

"No, no, he's doing better." Tess nodded approvingly at her husband. "He put his feet on the furniture the other day."

"Very funny." Nick tried to look supercilious, but his face collapsed into a grin when he looked at his wife.

Tess's grin reflected his. "Of course, it was a footstool, but still, I saw it as A Sign of Things To Come."

Mitch watched them and felt a pang at how comfortable they were together. Maybe commitment wouldn't be so bad if it was like this. And God knew, if people as different as by-the-book Nick and go-with-the-flow Tess could make it work, he could. With the right woman. If he ever found her. Not that he wanted to.

"Come to think of it, what are you doing here? If you're investigating the niece, I'm against it." Nick folded his arms. "I like her."

Tess nodded in agreement. "Me, too."

"So do I." Mitch sipped his drink to wash away the can-apé. "I'm working for her. How the hell did you ever end up fronting for Armand?"

"I was dating Mae, and she introduced us. I was trying to make points, so I said sure when he mentioned he had a little problem." Nick shook his head. "It seemed like a good idea at the time."

Tess and Mitch both looked at him with distasteful interest.

"Is there something wrong?" Nick said, looking from one to the other.

"You never told me you dated Mae," Tess said coolly.

"I never told you about a lot of the people I dated," Nick pointed out. "It was years ago. She'd just divorced that loser Dalton, and she was dating everybody, and my number came up. It was never serious. I didn't even know you then." He glared at Mitch. "And what's your problem? You're only working for her."

"I don't have a problem." Mitch glared back at his lawyer, noticing for the first time how damn good-looking he was. "No problem at all. What did you represent Armand for?"

"Fraud," Nick said.

"Get him acquitted?"

"Hell, no, he was guilty as sin. I had to work miracles to get him off with a fine and no jail time, and then he was mad because he was convicted." Nick scowled at the crowd in lieu of Armand. "He was a real piece of work, let me tell you."

Mitch frowned. "What kind of fraud?"

Nick hesitated and then shrugged. "It's public record. The whole thing was pretty convoluted, but what it came down to was that he'd looted a trust fund he'd been administering. The old lady who'd been living on the income from the fund got hot when it dried up and she sued. We managed to get him off with restitution and a fine, but it was close."

"What year?"

Nick gazed at him suspiciously. "Why are you so interested in this?"

"Mae has a trust fund. It appears to have fallen on hard times. What year?"

"It was 1989." Nick looked unhappy. "Tell me that Uncle Armand wasn't taking care of that fund for her."

Tess looked skeptical. "Would he be stupid enough to pull the same stunt twice?"

"Stupid, no. Greedy, yes. Armand Lewis would steal anything that wasn't nailed down. If he had a chance at her trust fund, he'd take it." Nick stopped, considering. "Of course, she's probably going to inherit everything, anyway."

"Maybe not," Mitch said. "There appears to be a wife."

Nick's jaw dropped. "He married Stormy?"

Tess moved in closer. "Who's Stormy?"

Nick put his arm around her. "Forget her. I never dated her. He married her?"

"Nope. Somebody named Barbara Ross." Mitch looked at him thoughtfully. "Why didn't you date Stormy?"

"Barbara Ross? That shellacked blonde from the Junior League?" Nick frowned, perplexed. "Not Armand's type at all."

"Why didn't you date Stormy?" Tess echoed.

"She said no." Nick's frown smoothed out. "I've got it. It was the money. Barbara Ross is old money. This was just Armand looking for cash again."

"She said no?" Tess's voice was full of amazement.

"Stormy was faithful to Armand," Nick told her. "She never cheated on him. God knows why."

"So who else did you ask out?" Tess pursued and Mitch went to Nick's rescue.

"Listen, any guy would try for Stormy. She's fantasy material."

"Is she?" Tess turned to her husband. "Tell me about it."

"I don't have to." Nick turned her gently around and pointed over her shoulder. "That's her. The redhead."

Stormy had drifted into the room, incandescent in a black lace suit. Every man in the room turned toward her.

"Oh," Tess said. "I see."

"I got to know her during the trial." Nick stood with his hand on Tess's shoulder, his mouth close to her ear, but Mitch could still hear him. "To tell you the truth, there's not much there. She's very nice, but . . ."

"She has the attention span of a fruit fly," Mitch finished. "I get the feeling she has a hard time remembering to mourn."

"Well, she's not the only one," Tess said. "Mae should have hired professional weepers for this gig."

"I thought about it," Mae said, and they all jumped.

"Don't sneak up on people like that, Mabel," Mitch groused. "It's rude."

Mae folded her arms. "I didn't sneak, I walked. If you hadn't been drooling over Stormy, you'd have seen me coming a mile away."

"I was not drooling," Mitch said with dignity. "I was observing."

"How very professional of you." Mae turned to the Jamiesons who were watching the byplay with interest. "Have you all been introduced?"

"Of course," Nick said before Tess could speak. "We've known Mitch Peatwick for years."

"Who?" Tess said.

"Peat-wick," Nick said, emphasizing the syllables.

"Absolutely," Tess said.

Mae blinked. "How do you know one another?"

Nick froze. "Uh, tell her, Mitch."

"I did some work for Nick," Mitch said, wondering how Nick got his reputation as the fastest lawyer in town if he couldn't think any faster than that.

"Right," Nick said.

Mae shook her head at Mitch. "If you think I'm buying that, you don't know me."

"I know you plenty." Mitch jerked his head toward June who was exiting with an empty tray. "I notice June is wearing her clothes again, not you."

Mae waved this away. "We share sometimes."

"I also notice they fit her."

Tess broke in. "So exactly how long have you known each other?"

"Three fun-filled days," Mae told her.

"You're kidding," Tess said.

"Oh, no." Mae looked past her, and they all turned to follow her eyes.

A tall, skeletally thin, blond woman draped in black crepe was posed in the doorway. She looked like death with big hair.

"That's Barbara," Mae said as she pushed past Mitch.

Nick moved to lean against the sideboard beside Mitch. "This should be good. Where'd you get that drink, anyway?"

"Take mine." Mitch handed it to him. "Somebody's going to have to head off Stormy." He moved away, hot on Mae's trail.

Tess joined her husband against the wall. "I find this all very interesting."

He smiled down at her. "Barbara and Stormy?"

"No. Mitch and Mae."

Nick watched Mitch cross the room to block Stormy's view as Mae steered Barbara in the opposite direction. "You think so?"

"No doubt in my mind," Tess said firmly.

"Then it must be true." Nick saw Mitch take Stormy's arm with all the enthusiasm he'd feel for a leper. "Poor Mitch. The last of the red-hot bachelors, doomed."

"Doomed?" Tess echoed ominously.

"To a life of wedded bliss," Nick added and put his arm around her.

"You make it sound boring," Tess said.

"Not with you." Nick's eyes went back across the room. "And not with Mae, either."

He started to laugh then and didn't stop until Tess elbowed him in the ribs.

"BARBARA, how lovely to see you," Mae burbled, trying to keep an eye out for Stormy.

"At such a terrible time," Barbara reminded her, offering her heavily made-up cheek to Mae.

Mae air-kissed her, which seemed to please her, and then shot a quick glance over her shoulder in time to see Mitch steering Stormy in the opposite direction. Mitch looked as unhappy as he looked determined, a knight in a really bad tie, and she felt a wave of affection for him roll over her.

"Such a terrible thing," Barbara was saying. "We'd been married just a little over a week."

"It must not seem real," Mae comforted her, not adding *it doesn't seem real to me.*

"Well, legally it's real." Barbara's eyes swept the room's contents. "My things will begin arriving on Monday."

"Things?" Mae echoed. "What things?"

"My furniture and things." Barbara's eyes narrowed. "I'll be moving in, of course."

"Of course." Mae tried to regroup. "Why?"

"Because this was Armand's house." Barbara's voice sharpened. "He'd want me to be here."

Mae repressed the impulse to point out that Armand was dead and even if he was watching them now, he probably didn't give a damn where she lived. Armand's interests had always centered solely on Armand. If there was an afterlife, Armand was scoping out the possibilities of after-profit, not worrying about his widow. And now that she'd spent a few minutes with Barbara, Mae wasn't sure why he'd wanted her around when he was alive. Of course, she had the Ross name. Old money. Just like Armand to acquire a wife with the equivalent of a label on her butt. Poor Stormy was generic, and Barbara was private brand.

Barbara's voice cut through her reverie. "This won't be a problem, will it, Mae?"

"Of course not." Mae smiled brightly at her. "I'll just alert June and Harold that you're coming."

"Fine. And give them two weeks' notice while you're at it." Barbara's eyes swept the room again. "I have my own help."

Mae clenched her teeth to keep from telling Barbara what she could do with her help. "Actually, Barbara, that would be a very bad idea. We can talk about this later, but for now, I'll just not mention the two weeks' notice."

Barbara opened her mouth, and Mae took her arm and moved her toward the front of the room. "After all, this is a memorial, not a discussion of Armand's assets. We must re-

member Armand now. Which reminds me, Uncle Claud will
want to see you." She smiled at Barbara coldly, not adding
to find out if you really married his brother. Let Claud handle that.

"We're brother and sister now, Claud." Barbara extended
her hand to the old man.

"Hello, Barbara," he said, taking her hand for a nano-
second before dropping it.

"I know you'll be glad to know that I'm moving here,"
Barbara went on, as if daring Mae to object. "It's what
Armand would have wanted."

Claud looked at Mae. "I will take care of this."

"She plans to fire Harold and June," Mae said. "I suggested that would be bad."

"Well, really, Mae." Barbara stared down her nose at her.

"Harold and June will stay," Claud said flatly.

"I fail to see the reason—"

Claud's voice cut across Barbara's. "Because that is what
Mae wants. Half of the equity in this house is yours. We will
work out suitable financial recompense."

"I don't want money." Barbara made cash sound like
something unclean. "I want to live in Armand's house, just
as he intended."

"Fine, I'll take the money," Mae said.

Claud's eyes slid to hers. "Is that what you want?"

"I don't like this house. Harold and June and I would be
happier somewhere else."

Claud's eyes panned back to Barbara's. "I will negotiate the
sale."

"I don't want to buy anything." Barbara sounded exasperated. "I'm Armand's widow. I don't have to buy anything."

"I'm missing something good, aren't I?" Mitch whispered in Mae's ear, and she jumped in surprise as his breath tickled her neck.

"Where's Stormy?" she whispered back.

"Some face in an expensive suit came and took her away from me." Mitch grinned at her. "I was so glad, I almost tipped him."

"And who is this?" Barbara did not sound amused.

Mitch turned to Barbara, and Mae could tell from the way he looked at her that he had her number immediately. He took her hand and pumped it. "Mitchell Peatwick. Sorry about your loss. When exactly did you marry Armand?"

"A week ago Monday in Barbados." Barbara answered automatically as she recovered her hand. "I don't believe I've had the pleasure of meeting you before."

"No," Mitch agreed. "Why did he come back on Friday in the middle of the honeymoon?"

Barbara's nostrils flared. "Really, Mr. Peatwick, I fail to see how that is any of your business."

Mitch beamed at her. "Oh, it's my business. Mabel hired me to look into his murder, so his movements the week before his death are definitely my business."

"His murder?" Barbara stiffened. "He wasn't murdered."

Mitch just smiled. "Say, you haven't seen his diary lately, have you?"

"Oh, look, there's Uncle Gio," Mae said brightly, and Mitch swung around and said, "Where?" She tugged on his sleeve, dragging him toward the door to the hall. "Come on."

"Great to have met you," Mitch called over his shoulder to Barbara. "What a trout," he said to Mae as soon as they were in the hall, out of earshot. "Was Gio really out there?"

"Yes, by the French doors with Carlo. Forget them. Barbara's the problem. She's planning on moving in and firing Harold and June."

Mitch winced at the thought. "I wouldn't want her for a roommate. Maybe that's why Armand died. He couldn't stand the thought of living with her."

"Why did he have to marry her?" Mae leaned against him for a moment, weighed down by another unexpected problem, and she felt comforted when he put his arm around her. "Now I have her to contend with, too." He felt so good, so solid, so warm next to her that she nestled against him a little and closed her eyes.

"You're not alone here, Mabel." Mitch's voice seemed huskier than usual as she felt his arm tighten around her. "You hired me, remember? We'll work something out."

Mae blinked. "We?"

"Yeah. You and me."

He smiled down at her, and Mae swallowed. She was so used to hearing, "I'll take care of it," and being told to run along and play, that Mitch's assumption they would handle the problem together caught her off guard. "I like you," she said. "I like you a lot."

Mitch's smile faded. "I like you, too. Are you all right?"

"Why?"

"Well, usually you're telling me what a loss I am. I'm not used to this side of you."

"Mae?"

She turned, startled to see her ex-husband, Dalton Briggs, standing in the doorway, as perfectly pressed and symmetrically handsome as ever, the epitome of a *GQ* cover. The contrast between him and Mitch couldn't have been greater.

She'd never appreciated Mitch more.

"Mae, I need to talk to you." Dalton smiled as his eyes slid over Mitch, obviously dismissing him as inconsequential. "Could we have a moment alone, please?"

Mitch tightened his arm around Mae again. "No." He scowled down at her. "First Carlo, then Nick, now this stiff. Don't you know any ugly men?"

"Stiff?" Mae blinked at him.

"I've been hanging around Harold too long. This is the face who snagged Stormy. Do we know him?"

"Mitchell Peatwick, Dalton Briggs," Mae said obediently.

Mitch shook his head in wonderment. "So this is Dalton the fool."

"I beg your pardon," Dalton said, his voice heavy with disapproval.

"Yes," Mae said.

"You actually married him."

"I was young," Mae said.

"Who are you?" Dalton asked Mitch, really looking at him for the first time.

"Go away," Mitch said to him. "That five hundred thousand meant you were supposed to disappear forever."

Dalton flushed. "I don't know who the hell you are, but—"

"Not now, Dalton." Mae moved away from Mitch's arm to go back into the dining room and away from this new crisis, whatever it was. "I've got a houseful of people for a memorial service. I can't deal with you now."

"We need to talk." Dalton took her hand as she moved past him. "I can stay after—"

Mitch tightened his grip on her other hand. "No, you can't."

"Listen, you," Dalton began.

"Tomorrow night," Mae said wearily. "Come by tomorrow night at six. I'll talk to you then, when this is all over." She didn't want to see Dalton, but seeing him was easier than wrangling in the hall.

"That is a bad idea," Mitch told her.

"I'll see you tomorrow night," Dalton said firmly, glaring at Mitch. "Alone."

"That is a really bad idea," Mitch said.

Mae opened her mouth to answer him but stopped when Stormy drifted out into the hall, her eyes glued to Mitch.

"Hello, Mitch, how are you?" she said, and Mae dropped Mitch's hand.

"I'm fine," he told her gently. "Are you all right?"

"Oh, yes. I'm going home with Dalton now." She smiled up at him. "But I want you to come see me, too. Do you know where I live?"

"I'll find out," Mitch promised.

Stormy tugged on Dalton's sleeve. "I'm ready to go now. I don't like this."

"All right." Dalton covered her hand with his. "I'll see you tomorrow night, Mae."

"Fine."

All Mae wanted was for everyone to leave. Especially Stormy. Everyone except Mitch. The rest of this crowd coul disappear in front of her eyes, and she'd only be grateful as long as she could still hang on to Mitch.

"I think I should be with you tomorrow night," Mitch said as soon as the pair were gone.

"What's with you and Stormy?" Mae asked, not wanting to fight about Dalton. "Have you adopted her?"

"I think that's what she's looking for. A daddy." Mitch leaned against the wall and watched her. "She's not like you. She wants somebody to make all the decisions for her."

Mae stopped. "What makes you think I don't want that?"

"The way you look like murder when anybody tries it." Mitch reached out and touched her cheek. "You look tired, Mabel. Why don't you go upstairs and take a nap? I'll tell everyone you were overcome with grief."

A nap sounded wonderful. Mae thought longingly of her big white bed upstairs, and then she thought longingly of Mitch in that big white bed with her. It wasn't even a carnal thought; she just wanted him to hold her. She tried not to dwell on the thought because if she did, it would become carnal and that would never work. The last thing she needed was carnal thoughts about somebody who needed to lay pipeline and open the West.

The big dummy.

She glared at him.

"What?" He blinked at her, surprised. "What did I say?"

"Nothing." Mae rubbed her hand over her forehead. "I'm having a rough day. Come on. Let's get this memorial over so people will go home." She turned back to the dining room.

"Fine," Mitch said as they joined the clutch of bored-looking mourners. "But I meant what I said about your not seeing Dalton alone. It would be bad."

"Why?" Mae moved deeper into the crowd, not really listening for his answer. It was time to get this show on the road, have a couple of people say nice lies about Armand and then get them all out of her house.

Or Barbara's house.

"You might miss something," Mitch was saying as he followed her. "He might say something that's a clue, and you'd miss it."

"I would not miss it." Mae stopped to scan the crowd. "Have you seen the minister? He was going to speak first."

"I am definitely going to be with you tomorrow. Dalton is—don't sneak up on me like that, damn it. It's antisocial."

"I didn't," Mae protested as she turned back to him, and then she stopped.

Carlo was standing beside Mitch, looking even more homicidal than usual. "You are not going to be with her to-morrow night," Carlo began.

"Don't even think about it, Carlo," Mae said. "I hired him, and I want him. Leave him alone."

Mitch scowled back at Carlo. "If you want to do something helpful, go beat up the widow. She's trying to evict Mae from the house."

Carlo swung around to Mae. "Is that true?"

"Uncle Claud is handling it," Mae stalled him.

A man in black appeared at the podium at the end of the room and rapped on it with his knuckles before Carlo could speak. "If you would all take your seats, I've been asked to say a few words about the departed. Then you may all share your thoughts with us."

People drifted into the chairs, most looking grimly determined not to share their thoughts. Carlo returned to Gio and whispered in his ear. Mae sat numbly through the minister's remarks, wincing only when he referred to Armand as "Almond," a mistake Mitch evidently found hilarious judging from the way his shoulders shook. Then the minister stepped back and invited others to speak. Mae had one moment of fear that no one would step forward, and then Barbara stood and made a queenly march to the front.

"Armand Lewis was my husband," she began, pausing only as the murmur of surprise swept the assembly. "And I loved him." She broke down then, and Mae said, "I don't feel well," and escaped out the side door.

The memorial went quickly after that. As Mitch remarked later, nobody could clear a room like Barbara Ross. Most of the people said vaguely comforting things as they sidled out the front door, but Tess Jamieson was the most help. "If all this starts to get to you," she told Mae, "call me. We'll rent videos and eat ice cream."

"That sounds wonderful." Mae turned to Nick to say goodbye, only to hear him say to Mitch, "You have to talk to

Newton for me. He won't let me buy into this tin mine in Bolivia."

"Tin mine?" Mae's eyes went to Mitch. "What do you know about tin mines?"

"Exactly as much as Nick does, which is nothing." Mitch glared at him. "Which is why he should listen to Newton. Tin mines. Grow up, Jamieson."

"Who's Newton?" Mae asked. "What's going on?"

"Newton is a mutual friend," Mitch said. "And Nick is leaving."

"Goodbye." Nick pulled Tess after him as he went out the door. "Let's not do this again sometime."

Tess laughed and blew Mitch a kiss.

"Tin mines?" Mae asked again, but there were more people to say goodbye to, and when they were all gone, Claud asked her to join him in the library with Barbara and Armand's lawyer for a discussion of Armand's assets.

"You may go," Claud told Mitch, and Mitch looked at Mae.

"Go or stay?" he asked her. "It's your call."

Mae thought of Claud and Barbara and the lawyer. "Stay. I know that's above and beyond the call of duty but—"

"Whatever you want, boss." Mitch took her arm. "Let's go hear what the lawyer has to say."

"He is unnecessary," Claud said, but Mae just shook her head and led them both to the library.

"THE WILL IN FORCE predates Armand's marriage," the lawyer began. "But under Ohio law . . ."

His voice droned on, and Mitch tuned him out, watching Mae instead. She looked tired. It had been a god-awful afternoon, of course, but it was more than that. Whatever it was that was getting to her was growing worse. And he didn't believe for a moment that it was Armand's death. She was worried about something, and on a guess, that something was money. Whatever else happened, she believed she had to take care of Harold and June. And she needed money for that, and Armand's estate was disappearing before her eyes, some of it stolen by Armand before he died, half of it stolen now by this Mayflower harpy with the plastic hair.

Which meant he was going to have to find out what happened to the things that Armand had taken.

Which probably meant that he was going to have to find the diary.

Mitch grinned. Mae Belle was going to get what she wanted, after all.

The lawyer droned on. ". . . and therefore, the will stands as is, with half of the assets devolving upon the widow, and the other half distributed as provided for in the will. Those provisions are as follows." The lawyer cleared his throat self-importantly. "Fifty thousand dollars each to June Peace and Harold Tennyson."

"Ridiculous," Barbara said.

"You're right," Mae said. "It should have been ten times that."

"One half of all stock held to Claud Lewis," the lawyer continued. "And the balance of the estate to Mae Belle Sullivan." He peered over his glasses at them all. "It's quite straightforward. However, there is a problem."

Claud's eyes flickered. "A problem?"

The lawyer cleared his throat again. "We are still investigating, of course, but the bank as executor and I . . ."

His voice trailed off again and Mitch sat up straighter, interested. This was one unhappy lawyer.

"Actually, there doesn't seem to be an estate," the lawyer said.

"What?" Mae said, and the lawyer looked miserable.

"As far as we can determine," he told her unhappily, "the only assets Mr. Lewis possessed were this house and its contents."

Claud remained silent. Mae took a deep breath and then was quiet. But Barbara began to talk immediately. "I can't believe it. Armand was a wealthy man. He had stock, investments...." She turned to Claud. "Surely you must know—"

"I purchased all his outstanding Lewis and Lewis stock. I have no knowledge of any of Armand's other assets." Claud stood and looked down at Mae. "Do not concern yourself about this. You and Harold and June will be taken care of." He nodded once to the lawyer and once to Barbara, and then he was gone.

Mae leaned back in her chair and covered her eyes with her hand.

"I want this house and its contents evaluated on Monday," Barbara announced to the lawyer.

"Miss Sullivan?" the lawyer said even more unhappily, and Mae waved her hand at him.

"Go ahead. I don't care."

"You have nothing to say about it," Barbara snapped.

"That's enough." Mitch stood up. "It's been a long day and Mae's tired. You can talk about this again on Monday."

"I'll talk about it now," Barbara said. "I want to—"

"Go home," Mitch said, and his voice was so firm and matter-of-fact that even Mae looked up. "Now."

Barbara opened her mouth and then must have thought better of it. She gathered up her things and swept out of the library, followed by the lawyer who practically ran her down trying to get away.

"Half the value of the house and its contents." Mae shook her head and swallowed. "It's not enough. It'll support them for four or five years, but not for the rest of their lives. They need enough for an annuity. I've got to find a way—"

Mitch sat down next to her and put his arm around her, alarmed at the quaver in her voice, cursing the chair arms between them. "So we'll find a way. Tomorrow. Tonight, we'll talk about something else. Just forget it all for right now. You sound like you're about ready to crack."

Bob peered through the open doorway and then padded into the room.

"You know, I really don't want to think about much of anything anymore." Mae's voice was heavy with fatigue.

"Then we'll talk about nothing. Tell me about Bob."

"About Bob?" Mae smiled and relaxed against him, and he closed his eyes briefly under the luxury of her weight. "There's not much to tell about Bob."

"Tell me what there is."

"I found Bob about seven years ago and brought him home to stay." Mae reached down and played with the dog's ears, sending him into ecstasy, and Mitch felt a moment's envy. That was bad. Envying a dog was not a good sign. "Armand hated him," Mae went on, still caressing the dog. "But I was twenty-seven, and it was harder to bully me than when I was a kid, so Bob stayed."

"I had a dog when I was a kid." Mitch watched the light gleam on her bent head, picking out the half circles of her dark curls. "A beagle. Of course, he was brighter than Bob. These chairs are brighter than Bob."

"I had a dog when I was a kid, too." Mae's smile faded as she straightened. "I found him on my way home from school. He was all skinny and hungry, and I brought him home, and June fed him, and we gave him a bath. He was beautiful, and we named him George."

"What kind was he?"

"All kinds. My kind. But George wasn't a pure breed, so when Armand got home, he took him to the pound."

"What?" Mitch tightened his hold on her. "That son of a bitch."

"I was hysterical," Mae went on, still playing with Bob's ears as she leaned against Mitch. "And Armand refused to go back and get George. So June called Uncle Gio because I wouldn't stop crying, and Uncle Gio said, 'Tell her I will fix it,' and June did, and I still cried myself to sleep. And the next day, June took me to Uncle Gio's, and George was there, and Uncle Gio promised me he'd always be there, and after that, I went to dinner every Sunday and played with George." Mae looked up at him, her eyes bright. "And that is why I do not believe that my Uncle Gio has ever hurt anybody, and why I still go to dinner every Sunday even though George died twelve years ago, and why I hated my Uncle Armand, and why I'm not sorry that he's dead."

Mitch pulled her out of her chair and into his lap, holding her close, his cheek against her hair, while she buried her face in his shoulder. "It's going to be all right," he said.

"I know," Mae said on a muffled sob. "I know. I'm just so tired."

"And maybe I was wrong about Gio," Mitch went on, closing his eyes again as he held her. "But your cousin Carlo is still for the birds."

She laughed into his shoulder then, and he relaxed into relief, but she was still tense when he finally left her.

He really hated leaving her.

6

"THIS IS SO NICE," Stormy told Mae the next day. She gazed in delight around the sedate lunchtime crush at the Levee. "I always feel so rich here." She was wearing a navy blue dress that was shirred across the shoulders and that made her look demure and sexy and refined and breathtakingly beautiful. Mae was wearing another of her flowered sundresses, this one pink, knowing it didn't really matter what she wore, anyway; she was invisible as long as she was sitting next to Stormy. "Don't you feel rich here?" Stormy asked her.

"No. This place always reminds me of how poor I am." Mae scanned the menu tiredly. "I'll have a small salad," she told the hovering waiter.

"Lobster." Stormy beamed at him. "I love lobster."

The waiter beamed back and left them, and Mae did some quick calculations to see how badly lunch was going to maim her financially.

"Armand didn't bring me here much." Stormy's smile faded, and her eyes brightened with incipient tears. "He liked it to be just us at home."

He liked it cheap, Mae amended silently, but all she said was, "That must have been nice."

"I like this better." Stormy looked around and began smiling again. "Dalton brought me here three times this week."

"So you're seeing Dalton," Mae said, trying to goose the conversation away from Armand and tears. "How nice."

Stormy leaned forward a little. "You don't mind, do you?"

"Mind what? That you're seeing Dalton?" Mae laughed. "Good heavens, no. Feel free."

"Well, he is your ex-husband," Stormy offered. "I thought maybe..."

"Take him with my blessings," Mae said firmly. "Dalton is definitely out of my life."

Stormy put her chin in her hand and surveyed Mae. "What about Mitch?"

"What about Mitch?" Mae echoed, suddenly not finding the conversation as amusing.

"Are you dating him?"

"No." Mae picked up a breadstick and crunched into it. "I'm employing him," she said when she'd swallowed. "That's it."

"Because I think he's really sexy." Stormy let her eyes roam the room again. "I don't know why. He's not very handsome. Dalton is handsome."

"Date them both and split the difference." Mae tried to keep the annoyance out of her voice. It was a good thing that Stormy was interested in Mitch since it was inevitable that Mitch in turn would be interested in Stormy. It meant that she wouldn't have to worry about all of the problems that might develop if she gave in to her baser instincts and made a pass at him. *He didn't seem too thrilled with her yesterday*, a little voice inside her offered, but she squelched it. If Stormy turned those big blue eyes on him, Mitch would fall. Any man would. Especially a man who needed to lay pipeline and open the West. "He's all yours," she told Stormy and crunched into her breadstick again.

"Well, I don't know. I'm seeing a couple of other guys, too. I just met one yesterday—" Stormy stopped as the waiter served their salads. "Thank you."

The waiter stopped, stunned by her smile.

Mitch wasn't going to have a chance. Mae sighed and stabbed her salad.

"None of them are like Armand, though," Stormy said when the waiter was gone, and Mae resisted the urge to point out that this was a definite plus. "They keep asking me what I want to do. Armand just told me. That was nice. Sort of."

Mae chewed faster to keep from blurting out her opinion.

"I mean, that's how I knew he loved me." Stormy poked at her salad listlessly. "He took care of me. You know? Isn't that what every woman wants?"

"No." Mae put down her fork. "Didn't you ever want to make the decisions?"

"No." Stormy blinked at her. "Not very much. It was like Armand said, his way, everything was a surprise. It was like Christmas, only everyday."

"But what if you didn't want to do what Armand wanted to?" Mae persisted. "What if you wanted to do something else?"

Stormy's eyes shifted away from hers. "Why would I want to do something else? Like Armand said, that's what love is, having somebody take care of you. Armand knew what was best." She put down her fork and fumbled inside her purse to pull out a small jeweled box. "I liked it that way," she said defiantly. She popped a tiny white pill in her mouth. "It was best."

"Not for me." Mae thought of her car and a thousand other things Armand had overruled her on for her own good. "For me, love is a partnership. Making decisions together."

"That's dumb." Stormy dropped the box back into her purse and went back to her salad. "If a guy will take care of you, let him."

"And then what happens when he's gone?" Mae stopped with her fork in midair. "What happens when he leaves you high and dry?"

"Armand didn't leave me." There was an edge to Stormy's voice. "Armand *died*."

"Armand married Barbara Ross."

Stormy flushed and looked more beautiful than ever. "He wasn't leaving me. He bought me my own place and gave me money so I'd feel secure, but he wasn't leaving me. He loved me."

Mae bit back the impulse to say, *"He married another woman, how is that love?"* and said instead, "So what are you going to do now?"

Stormy cocked her head, looking about as thoughtful as she ever got. "Well, there's Dalton. He's fun and rich, and he wants to take me on vacation, but he's no Armand. And then I met this new guy yesterday, and he's sweet and rich. And then there's Mitch."

"Mitch is broke," Mae put in and then kicked herself.

"I know, but he's . . ." Stormy furrowed her brow. "He's safe. You know? He makes me feel good."

"Then go for it." Mae stabbed her salad again. "Money isn't everything."

"Oh, I wouldn't give up the money. I'd have to see Dalton or somebody else, too."

Mae put down her fork. "You'd two-time Mitch?"

Stormy blinked at her. "Do you think he'd care?"

Mae thought of Mitch and his "everybody lies" outlook on life. "No. I think he'd expect it." She felt sorry for him suddenly, spending the rest of his life with a woman who would only reinforce his lousy philosophy. Well, she wasn't any better than Stormy. She'd lied through her teeth to him about Armand being murdered.

"Why did he say that Armand was murdered?" Stormy asked and Mae jumped at the unexpected echo of her thoughts.

"What?"

"Why did Mitch say Armand was murdered? He wasn't. I was there." Stormy set her mouth into a stubborn line. "He wasn't murdered."

A tactful woman would have said "of course not," but Mae wasn't a tactful woman. "His diary is missing. It's important, and it's gone, and we figured that whoever has it murdered him to get it. Of course, if the diary turns up, that blows that theory out of the water, but it hasn't turned up. So we're looking for the diary." Mae watched her to see if there was any flash of recognition or guilt in her eyes, but there wasn't anything in Stormy's eyes except endless blue depths.

"That's dumb," Stormy said, and since basically she was right, Mae went back to pick at her salad. "Maybe Dalton will bring me here for dinner tonight," Stormy went on. "I'd like that."

"Suggest it," Mae said, exasperated.

Stormy blinked at her, not comprehending.

"Never mind." Mae thought gloomily of Mitch. He'd better develop ESP fast if he was going to keep Stormy. She put down her fork and stared in misery at her salad.

"You're not eating your lunch," Stormy said.

"I'm not very hungry," Mae said.

AT FOUR-THIRTY that afternoon, Mitch ran down the stairs of his apartment building, determined to be upbeat that night for Mae's sake, even though he'd spent the day talking to everyone who'd ever known Armand Lewis to see if they'd noticed anything unusual about him lately.

They had. He'd been selling everything he owned. Evidently, the lawyer hadn't been exaggerating the night before. If the rumors he'd been picking up were true, Armand's assets were exactly the house and its contents. He'd even sold his classic BMW for $250,000. Armand had had one hell of a garage sale, after all.

Mitch pushed through the street door rehearsing exactly how he was going to drop this bomb on Mae, but he stopped when he saw his car.

All the tires were slashed again, but this time, Jack the car ripper had gone after the seats, too. "Top of the line K mart seat covers," Mitch said regretfully, and then he went back inside and called his mechanic, his insurance agent and the police. His mechanic said, "Somebody really hates you, Kincaid," and promised to come get the car. His insurance agent said, "You know, Mitch, this isn't going to look good on your insurance history," and promised to file the claim. The desk sergeant at the police station said, "Did you ever think of parking it anyplace else?" and began to make out the report.

"Got any idea who's doing this to you?" the sergeant said as he took down the information.

"Oh, maybe." Mitch thought grimly of Carlo. "Let me get back to you on this."

"Well, don't wait too long," the sergeant said. "Next time, it could be you instead of the tires and seats."

"Yes, but think how relieved my insurance agent would be," Mitch said, and hung up to call a cab.

"DID YOU EVER LOOK behind these books for the diary?" Mitch asked when he was standing in the library with Mae an hour later. She was glad to see him, and his sudden enthusiasm about the diary was touching in its way, but mostly she just wanted to get the rest of the day over with. "I think we should pull them out and—"

"Dalton is going to be here in a half hour." Mae slumped down into a chair. "Do whatever you want, but I've got to talk to him."

Mitch pulled a step stool over to the first bank of shelves. "I love libraries. Some of my best moments have been in libraries."

Mae regarded him wearily. "Why do I get the feeling that we're not talking about great books here?"

"Okay, so I like women who read." Mitch pulled out a section of books and felt behind them. "These books are all pushed flush with the wall. Do you see any that are sticking out a little?"

Mae surveyed the shelves. "No. How much reading did these women do?"

"A lot. Most of them were librarians." Mitch put the books back and climbed down. "If you were Armand, where would you put the diary?"

"I'd take it with me. What do you mean, librarians?"

"The first woman I ever loved was a library aide in high school." Mitch scanned the shelves. "Connie. She was perfect. We never argued, and she always went along with whatever I wanted, and we had incredible sex. I've been trying to find a woman just like her ever since." He frowned at Mae. "Where would he have taken it to?"

"The diary? Probably the town house. So why didn't you stay with Connie?" Mae asked, trying to squelch the annoyance in her voice.

"We went to different colleges, and it just sort of faded away. It was great. Incredible sex until we got bored with each other, and then we just said goodbye. I never found anyone like her again." He shook his head at Mae. "We searched the town house. The diary's not there."

"So what happened next?"

"We came back here," Mitch said, clearly puzzled.

"No, what happened next with the librarians?"

Mitch looked uncomfortable. "Could we talk about the diary?"

Mae folded her arms. "Later. Who came after Connie?"

Mitch sighed. "Daphne. She was a library major, working the college stacks, and she dropped some books and I picked them up. We were together for two years. Now, about the diary—"

"What happened?"

Mitch gave up. "She wanted to get married, and I said no, and she left. I couldn't believe it. Marriage. She must have been out of her mind." He frowned at the shelves. "That damn diary has to be somewhere, and I bet we've been where it is. Come on, Mabel, think."

"And after Daphne, there was . . ."

"What?"

"After Daphne . . ."

"Oh. Susan."

"Another librarian."

Mitch nodded. "Daphne introduced us."

"And what happened to Susan?"

"After a couple of years, she wanted to get married, too. Let's go upstairs and look in that box of Armand's stuff that Harold brought back from the town house."

"The diary isn't there. So what happened then?"

"To the diary?"

"No, to Susan," Mae said with obvious patience.

"She married a chiropractor six months later. It's got to be here, or at the town house, or at Stormy's condo, or with Barbara. Armand didn't go anyplace else. Except Barbados." Mitch frowned. "Are you sure he had the diary when he came back from Barbados?"

"He seemed to think so on the phone that night. So who came after Susan?"

Mitch scowled at her. "Rachel. Can we talk about something else?"

"No. Was Rachel another librarian?"

"No, she had a cable TV show."

"Ah, a break in the pattern. What kind of show?"

"It was called *Book Chat*," Mitch said with an attempt at dignity that turned into a grin when Mae laughed out loud. "So I like literate women. Big deal."

"And what happened to Rachel?"

"She wanted to get married," Mitch said. "Could we get back to the diary now?"

"Exactly how many librarians did you love and lose when they wanted to get married?"

"I have no idea. About the diary—"

"Count." Mae's voice was an order, so Mitch sighed and began ticking them off on his fingers, silently.

"Nine," he said finally.

"How many actually were librarians?"

"Seven."

Mae shook her head. "I can't believe it. You're a human Bob."

Mitch scowled at her. "I beg your pardon."

"When Bob was a puppy, June was cutting a steak on the counter, and it slipped and fell on the floor, and Bob grabbed it and ran into the library and swallowed it whole. It was the high point of his life. He threw it up on the library carpet about five minutes later, but it was still the high point."

"If you're comparing my relationship with Connie to swallowing a steak whole, I'm going to be annoyed."

"Since then," Mae went on as if she hadn't heard him, "Bob has sat by that counter waiting for another steak, even though June doesn't cut them there anymore. He's been sitting there for seven years, bashing his head against the cabinet, waiting for a steak that isn't there anymore." She shrugged. "You're a human Bob."

"If you're through amusing yourself with faulty analogies," Mitch said distantly, "I think we ought to look for the diary."

Harold appeared in the doorway. "That stiff Dalton is here."

"Show him in," Mae said. "Let's get this over with."

"A human Bob," Mitch said. "Thank you *very* much."

FOR ONCE, Mitch agreed with Harold completely: Dalton was a stiff. He came in looking immaculate and not quite real. Mitch watched Mae to see how she reacted, jealously documenting the way she stood to greet him, the way she gave him her hand, the way she didn't smile at him. She was doing pretty well, considering the guy was rich and good-looking and obviously wanted her.

Mitch sat down, depressed by his own inadequacies. Okay, so he wasn't exactly broke—once the bet was over, he could go back to living like a stockbroker—but he wasn't in Dalton's financial league and never would be. And he was also never going to look magazine-smooth like Dalton, which normally didn't bother him at all but was now bothering him significantly. Look at the guys Mae hung out with: Carlo, Nick, Dalton—hunks every one.

"No, Mitch stays," he heard Mae say to Dalton, and he jerked his attention back to the situation at hand.

"What I have to say is personal." Dalton looked deep into her eyes.

"Why don't you sit down?" Mitch growled at him. "She's tired. Cut her a break."

Dalton turned to him. "I need to see Mae alone. I'm sure you understand."

"No, I don't." Mitch crossed his arms and leaned back in his seat. "I'm staying."

"Dalton." Mae's voice cut across their antagonism. "Just tell me what you have to tell me and go. I'm really tired."

Dalton hesitated and then surrendered. He took her hand and said, "I think we should try it again, Mae."

Mitch swallowed hard.

Mae blinked at Dalton. "Try what? Marriage?"

"Of course, marriage." Dalton smiled down at her. "You silly. Of course, marriage."

"Not in this lifetime," Mae said flatly. "If that was what you wanted to see me about, you can go now."

"Mae, I know we made mistakes—"

"We didn't. You did." Mae glared at him. "You took half a million to dump me, and as I understand it, you did quite well with it. Well, now you can cuddle up to your cash because you're not getting me back."

"Mae, I was a fool—"

"You sure as hell were," Mitch growled. "Now get out."

Dalton turned to glare at Mitch, but Mae forestalled him. "He's right. If that was your message, you can leave."

"That wasn't all of it." Dalton's glare went out like a light, and the look he turned on Mae was sincerely sympathetic. "I'm sorry about this, Mae. I really am. I just heard today that all Armand left you was the house and its contents."

"I'll get by," Mae said stiffly.

"No, you won't," Dalton said without a hint of gloating in his voice. "Armand sold me the house and its contents last week. The money's been transferred. I don't know what he did with the money, but the house is gone. It's mine. He didn't leave you anything."

Mae took a deep breath, as if she'd had the air knocked out of her. "He sold you the house last week," she repeated.

"I'm sorry, Mae." Dalton's face was miserable. "But he got the money. The money must be somewhere."

Mitch watched her, wanting to go to her, knowing she'd want to handle things herself. He could have killed Dalton for doing this to her, but in all fairness, it wasn't Dalton's fault. It was Armand's. Before, he'd disliked Armand because of his general rotten behavior; now he loathed him for a good and present reason—he was torturing Mae from the grave.

If he'd been alive, Mitch would have killed him.

"Thank you for telling me, Dalton," Mae said faintly.

"Mae, my offer still stands." Dalton put his hand on her shoulder. "I'll take care of you and June and Harold. I promise. I've learned a lot since we broke up. I'm not the same guy I was. Give me a chance."

Mae blinked up at him, and Mitch closed his eyes. It was a decent offer. Dalton was trying to do the decent thing. It would get Mae out of all of her troubles and save June and Harold. All he was asking for was a chance.

Mitch wanted to kill Dalton, too.

"No," he heard Mae say firmly, and his world swung back into place. "I'm sorry, but no. You'd better go now. You're going to be late for your dinner with Stormy."

Dalton flinched and gave up.

Mae walked Dalton to the door, and Mitch waited for her to come back, trying to figure out what had happened to him in the past half hour. Here he was, sweating out Mae marrying another man. Big deal. He didn't want to marry her. He didn't want to marry anybody.

What would it have been like married to Mae? And what kind of a fool was Dalton to have taken money to leave her? He remembered the pain in Mae's voice when she'd thrown that at Dalton, and he hated the pain because it meant that she still hurt from something Dalton had done to her seven years ago.

He didn't want her to remember anything about Dalton. Or his damn check.

He reached in his jacket and pulled out his wallet, riffling through the papers and bills he'd jammed in there until he found Claud's check. He ripped it in half, and the halves in half, and the quarters in half, continuing until the pieces were tiny. Then he let them fall from his hand into the ashtray on the table beside him. He'd never meant to cash it, anyway, just to use it as a bargaining chip with Claud, but as a bargaining chip it was too expensive if it hurt Mae the way Dalton had hurt her.

She came back into the room then, the skirt of her sundress swinging slowly back and forth over her long, strong legs, and Mitch watched her with hypnotic interest.

He really didn't want to marry her. He just wanted to watch her move for the rest of his life.

"Are you okay?" he asked her when she was standing in front of him.

"This has got to be the bottom." Mae's voice was dead. "We've lost everything."

Mitch ached to pull her into his arms. "We can try to find the stuff that disappeared. I checked around today, and the rumors are that he was selling a lot of stuff. Get me a list of the things that are missing, and I'll try to track down the sales for you. And we can look for the money. It must be somewhere. Even if he bought something with it—stamps, gold, real estate, whatever—that's got to be somewhere."

"I can't think anymore." Mae smiled weakly down at him. "I'm going to bed, Mitch. I just can't think anymore. Can we talk about this some other time?"

He stood up. "I'll call you tomorrow." He put his hand on her cheek. "We're going to figure this out. Trust me."

Mae nodded, her cheek moving softly against his hand. "I know we will. I trust you. Call me in the evening. I go to Uncle Gio's tomorrow for Sunday dinner." She nodded again, her eyes looking up at him, huge as saucers. "Call me in the evening."

"In the evening." Mitch leaned forward and kissed her forehead, feeling awkward and foolish, hating it that he was leaving her, hating it that they were both alone. "Get some sleep. Tomorrow we'll get this right."

WHEN MAE WENT back into the library to put back the last of the books, she found a pile of paper scraps in the ashtray. And when she had them reassembled into Claud's check, she put her head down on the arm of the chair and cried, for no particular reason that she could think of.

"SO, HOW ARE THINGS, Mae Belle?" Gio asked the next day over lasagna for forty. There were only three of them, but Mae knew that Gio didn't like the idea of being caught short at Sunday dinner. If Mae Belle suddenly wanted to eat herself into a coma, he wanted to be ready.

"Fine," Mae said automatically, knowing that she was supposed to be eating herself into a coma but not finding the energy to do it. Most Sundays she tried, just to please Gio because she loved him, but this Sunday her heart wasn't in it.

"Then why are you picking at your food? She's picking at her food, Carlo. What's wrong, Mae? You can tell us." Gio peered at her anxiously. "I don't want you worrying, baby. You can tell us."

"It's that Peatwick jerk," Carlo rumbled.

"No, it's not the Peatwick jerk," Mae said irritably. "In fact, he's been wonderful. It's Armand."

"Armand is dead," Gio said.

"Yes, but before he died, he sold everything he had including the house, and now the money had disappeared. It's gone." Mae felt her voice quaver and stuck out her chin. "So Mitch and I are looking for it. And when we find it, everything will be fine."

"Mae, you want money, I'll give it to you," Gio said. "How much do you want?"

Mae shook her head. "I don't want you to give me money, although I may have to ask you to take on Harold and June. I can't afford to keep them if I don't find the money."

Gio scowled. "What happened to your trust fund? You get that pretty soon, don't you?"

"It's gone," Mae told him. "Uncle Armand told me that most of it had gone in some bad investments years ago."

Gio's face went hard. "Armand told you that?"

Mae shrugged. "I checked when he told me. He was right. There was only a couple of thousand left."

Gio sat back. "I wish that bastard wasn't dead so I could kill him myself."

Mae shook her head. "Just because my trust fund is empty, it doesn't necessarily mean that Armand stole it. And besides, it doesn't matter. It's gone. What matters is finding what happened to the money and the stuff that's disappeared lately. Mitch is looking for it, and if it can be found, he'll find it. He never gives up. Mitch makes pit bulls look flighty."

Carlo scowled at her from his end of the table.

"He takes good care of me, Carlo," Mae said soothingly. "And he never makes a pass. Never. He's a good detective."

"Does Claud know about the trust fund?" Gio's voice was short and cold, not the usual warm honey that flowed over her.

Mae blinked. "I suppose so. I never discussed it with him."

"Hmmph." Gio's eyes went to Carlo. "Armand."

"I know," Carlo said. "I told you we should have—"

"Never mind," Gio broke in. He turned back to Mae. "This P.I. He's not giving you any trouble?"

"I told you." Mae's voice was patient. "He's wonderful. He's funny and kind and smart and hardworking, and he never makes a pass, and he's doing everything he can to help me. He's wonderful." She stared down sadly at her lasagna.

Gio exchanged glances with Carlo. "Well, that's good. You let us know if he gets out of line."

"He won't get out of line," Mae said glumly. "He's a real gentleman."

"I'm going to kill him," Carlo said.

Mae looked up, startled. "Why?"

"It's just a figure of speech," Gio told her. "Just an expression." He glared at Carlo.

Mae cast a wary eye at Carlo. "Don't do anything, Carlo. I mean it."

Carlo frowned at his lasagna.

"Have some more lasagna," Gio said, heaping more on Mae's already laden plate. "It's good for you."

"I mean it, Carlo," Mae said.

"Eat!" Gio told her, and Mae picked up her fork and began to work her way through three pounds of lasagna.

"THERE'S TOO MUCH stuff missing, Newton," Mitch said over his own lunch that same Sunday.

"Why can't we eat someplace better than this?" Newton surveyed the clean, bright, plastic surroundings with distaste.

"Because this is what I can afford. Eat your Big Mac. You know you like it. You're just being a snob." Mitch bit into his sandwich, trying to ignore the fact that there wasn't enough room for his legs under the table.

"You've won the bet," Newton persisted. "You don't have to live like this anymore."

Mitch swallowed. "I like living like this. Now, concentrate. What would Armand have done with the stuff? Or with the money from the stuff."

Newton's eyes glazed over as he thought, and as he did, he absentmindedly bit into his sandwich, chewed and swallowed. "The missing items are paintings, antiques and collectibles, correct?"

"Correct."

"If he sold them, there will be a record of the sales. Try antique dealers, art galleries, known collectors. If you can't find any record of sales, look for well-guarded storage facilities and bank deposit boxes."

"And if I find out he's sold the stuff?"

"You know where to look. Swiss bank accounts, real estate purchases, bonds." Newton shook his head. "This doesn't make sense, Mitch. He wasn't planning on absconding. He was married. His position in the community meant a lot to him. If he were the type to swindle people and then go to Rio, I'd say that was what he was up to, but not Armand Lewis. He'd stay where being a Lewis meant something. It makes no sense that he'd be liquidating his estate."

"What if he was being blackmailed?" Mitch suggested. "What if he was paying somebody to keep his mouth shut?"

Newton shook his head. "Not Armand Lewis. He was used to risk. Not unless whoever it was had something that would really ruin him. Something that would put him in jail, for instance."

Mitch nodded. "Like the diary. The only problem is, he seems to have had the diary the night he died, and he'd been liquidating the estate for a couple of months. And if he was being blackmailed, it would make no sense to kill him. He'd be the goose that laid the golden eggs."

"Do you really think someone murdered him?" Newton sounded incredulous. "I thought that was Mabel's fantasy."

"Mabel is not a stupid woman." Mitch's voice was defensive. "Although I'm not even sure she really believes that he was murdered. She has ways that are murky. But there is something wrong here. Really wrong. And she's stuck in the middle of it." He looked at his sandwich, his appetite gone. "I think she's in trouble, Newton. I'm pretty sure that son of a bitch stole her trust fund. Unless I find out what he did with the cash he had, she's broke."

"Maybe she found out about the trust fund and killed him." Newton bit into his sandwich and missed the glare Mitch shot at him.

"Mabel did not kill her uncle. Gio might have if he'd had the chance. That quarter of a million must still rankle. Carlo would have killed him in a minute for turning him in to the police. Even Claud might have killed him to keep the family name from the gutter. But Mabel? Not a chance. She's a good woman, Newton."

Newton blinked at him. "I thought she was Brigid."

Mitch gazed at him in disgust. "Mabel is not Brigid. Stormy might be, though."

"Stormy doesn't have the concentration to be Brigid," Newton said flatly.

Mitch raised an eyebrow. "You've met Stormy?"

Newton shrugged. "Briefly. She's quite . . ."

"Harebrained?"

"Brains aren't everything."

Mitch shook his head in disbelief. "She got to you, too. I thought you'd be immune."

"Nonsense," Newton said.

And then he grinned.

MITCH CALLED MAE that night, but June told him she was sleeping. "I'm worried, Mitch," she said. "She's never like this. She's just worn-out with worry. You'll take care of it, won't you?"

"Yes," Mitch said, knowing that Mae would go ballistic at the thought of anyone taking care of her.

Well, what she didn't know wouldn't hurt her.

ON MONDAY, Mitch picked up his car and began to track down Armand in earnest, checking in at every art gallery and antique store he could find. As the day grew late, his list grew longer. Armand had been to most of the places, and most had bought from him or knew someone who had.

Somewhere, Armand had stashed a hell of a lot of money.

His last call was at Stormy's condo, and she was delighted to see him.

"I can only stay a minute," he began, but she pulled him down beside her onto a huge overstuffed sofa and leaned into him, and for one confused moment, Mitch wasn't sure which was sofa and which was Stormy, there was so much softness pressing against him.

"I'm so glad you're here," Stormy breathed into his neck, and Mitch winced and pulled away a little. Her perfume was exotic, and a week ago he'd have been breathing deeply, but lately, he'd developed a preference for women who smelled like soap.

"I just have a couple of questions about Armand," he told her, and she leaned closer again. He felt her softness give against him and wondered once more why Armand had ever left her for Barbara. Then he wondered why he was wondering that instead of enjoying the experience of having Stormy climbing up his arm.

Stormy was evidently wondering the same thing; she pulled away from him, confusion evident in her eyes.

"Did Armand leave anything here?" he asked her. "A box, maybe, or an envelope?"

"No."

Stormy flounced a little on the sofa and everything shifted under her sweater, and Mitch noted it with appreciation and moved on. She was fun to look at, but she wasn't Mabel. "Did he leave—"

"He was never here," Stormy said impatiently. "All his stuff is at the town house. Harold packed up Armand's clothes in boxes, and put his stuff that wasn't clothes in another box, and threw out all his underwear and socks, and took the things in the box home with him, and that's all there was. Armand was never here. I like you a lot."

"Good," Mitch said absentmindedly. "I like you, too. Did he—"

Stormy's lips closed on his as she slithered into his lap, and his arms went around her automatically as all her pneumatic roundness pressed against him. "Mae said it was okay," she breathed into his ear.

"She said what?" Mitch said, outraged, and then Stormy kissed him again, and he concentrated on getting out of her octopus embrace so he could go yell at Mae for setting him up. He pulled his lips away from hers with an audible pop. "No. I'm really flattered, Stormy, but Mae lied. It's not okay."

Stormy slipped off his lap and onto the couch beside him. "Are you sure? She seemed sure."

Mitch stood up before she could leap on him again. "I'm sure. Listen, if you remember anything that Armand left behind, call me—uh, Mae. Call Mae, please. It's important."

Stormy frowned up at him. "Usually, men really like kissing me."

"And I did, too," Mitch assured her. "Absolutely. Well, I gotta go now." He beat a hasty retreat to the door, wondering in the back of his mind why he was fool enough to leave this beautiful woman, and knowing in the back of the back of his mind exactly why he was leaving her.

He was seeing too much of Mabel. She was clouding his thought processes, and he didn't have many to begin with. That was going to have to stop.

He got into his car and checked his watch. He was meeting Mae at eight, and he was definitely going to have to shave and shower before then so she couldn't smell Stormy's perfume on him. Not that she'd care. She'd told Stormy that it would be okay to rape him on a couch. Well, the hell with her. He wasn't even going to dress up to see her. He didn't care, either. Jeans and an old T-shirt, that would show her.

He sighed as he drove toward his apartment. Somehow, lately, all his thoughts of Mabel were depressing. He was definitely going to have to solve this case and stop seeing her.

But first, he had to see her.

7

MAE MET HIM at the door, telling herself she was being polite, not overeager. She'd deliberately dressed in an old white T-shirt and jeans, just to show herself that she didn't care what he thought. He was dressed in an old white T-shirt and jeans, too. She wasn't sure what that meant, but she was so glad to see him that she didn't care.

"Hello, Mabel. Nice T-shirt," he said and she stood back to let him in, enjoying the fact that he was there and kicking herself for enjoying it.

"What did you find out?" she asked, trailing him into the library.

Mitch sat down and looked at her with sympathy, and she knew it was going to be bad. "He sold it all. I can't tell you if I tracked down everything until I get a look at your list, but I found where he offloaded most of the stuff you'd mentioned, like the Lempicka and the chess set."

Mae sank into a chair across from him. "So where's the money?"

Mitch sighed. "I looked. As far as I can tell, he doesn't have a stash. I even went to Stormy's new place—"

"Did you?" Mae said coolly.

"And she didn't know anything either. Which shouldn't have come as a surprise, somehow. Is she naturally dopey or does she have chemical assistance?"

"So how is Stormy?" Mae asked, steel in her voice.

"She's fine." Mitch seemed suddenly wary.

"Really." Mae tightened her lips. "How fine is she?"

Mitch blinked at her. "What are you talking about?"

"Don't play dumb." Mae scowled at him. "I've seen your real dumb, and this is not it. How was she in bed?"

"What?"

Mae began to tap her foot. "I said, how was she in bed?"

Mitch tried to look injured and innocent. "I wouldn't know."

"She didn't make a pass at you?"

"Of course not." Mitch swallowed.

"You're lying."

"Everybody lies. Except me. Can we talk about something else?"

"No. I'm paying for this information." Mae took a deep breath. "Did you sleep with her?"

"No." Mitch scowled at her. "Not that it's any of your business, boss, but no, I didn't."

Mae blinked at him. "You know, I believe you."

"Thank you."

She sat back in her chair, irrationally relieved. "So what was the problem? Was it a lousy pass?"

"No." Mitch surrendered. "It was a great pass. She's a very warm woman."

"Hot," Mae corrected.

"Throbbing," Mitch agreed.

"So what went wrong? Was it because she wasn't a librarian?"

Mitch shrugged. "I wasn't."

"Wasn't what? A librarian?"

"Throbbing." Mitch sank down a little into his seat. "Could we talk about something else?"

"No. Why weren't you throbbing?"

"Well, I'm not sure." Mitch's exasperation was apparent. "I think you've made me impotent."

"Oh." Mae smiled complacently. "That's nice."

Mitch shot her a nasty look. "My day rate just doubled."

Mae ignored him. "So she couldn't make you throb, huh?"

"I was concentrating on my work. Nobody makes me throb when I'm working. I'm a pro." Mae smiled at him, and he shifted uncomfortably in his chair. "Forget it, cookie. You're not my type. Now can we get back to Armand?"

"Sure." Mae felt cheerful for the first time in days. "What do you want?"

"I want to see that box of Armand's things that Harold brought back from the town house."

Mae shook her head. "Mitch, there's nothing in there. I looked, Harold looked—"

"And now I want to look. Do you want to sit here and explain to me why I don't need to look at the box before we go get it, or do you want to just cut to the chase and go get it?"

Mae sighed. "I'll go get it."

"Good for you, Mabel." Mitch nodded at her approvingly. "You're learning. Slowly, but you're learning."

"THERE'S NOTHING in here," Mitch said fifteen minutes later when they were both sitting on the floor peering into the big cardboard box.

Mae bit her lip to keep from saying I told you so.

"A thousand condoms, a hundred Chap Sticks, a bottle of heart pills, a bottle of aspirin, a roll of antacids, three pens and a calculator." Mitch stirred the mess with his finger.

"You're exaggerating on the condoms and Chap Sticks." Mae watched his hands move the contents of the box. "But there are a lot of them. Why would Armand want so many?"

"Maybe he was an optimist. Maybe his lips were really dry." He picked up the pill bottle and read the label. "Digoxin." He handed the bottle to Mae. "Do these look right to you?"

Mae took the bottle and popped the lid off, dumping a few of the white pills onto her palm. "I guess so. I never really paid much attention to them. The color's right."

Mitch pawed through the box again as she put the lid back on the bottle and tossed it back in. "Ah-ha! What's this?" He held up a small key with a blue plastic head and smiled at it with such delight that Mae was taken aback.

"It's not a safe-deposit key," Mae said. "Harold checked everywhere. Nobody he asked knew what it was."

"It's a storage-shed key." Mitch sat back, smug. "To the best high-security storage facility in Riverbend. It's about two miles from here."

Mae blinked at him. "And how do you know that?"

"I'm a detective. I detected it." He stood up. "Come on. This could be it."

"I don't believe this." Mae sat stubbornly at his feet. "How did you know that?"

"Fine, sit there." Mitch stepped over her. "I'm going to go find Armand's money, but you'd rather sit on the floor."

"All right, all right." Mae scrambled to her feet. "I'm coming. But I still don't believe this. You're keeping something from me."

"I should be so lucky," Mitch said.

Mitch's gas tank was on empty, so they stopped for gas, and when it turned out that Mitch's wallet was on empty, too, Mae forked over her last twenty.

"We'd better find the mother lode in this storage shed," she told him. "That's my lunch money for a week."

"We'll stop at an ATM on the way back. Trust me."

"Right," Mae said.

The storage facility, when they got there, was on a back street of one of Riverbend's better areas, tucked in among condos and apartment houses and hidden by trees and shrubs as if it were some less fortunate architectural relative. Mae saw dozens of sheds as they pulled up to the gate, all lined up in little streetlike rows labeled with white signposts, the sheds painted a refined stone blue and topped with white-gabled roofs. They looked like condos for elves.

"Hey, Mitch, how's it goin'?" the man at the gate said, and Mitch said, "Fine, Albert. What's happening?"

Albert snorted. "Nothing. That's why you pay us a fortune, so nothing happens to your stuff."

"Right," Mitch said, and Albert passed him through like a long-lost brother.

Mae fumed. So Mitch was paying a fortune for an upscale storage shed, was he? All right. That was it. Whatever Mitchell Peatwick was, he wasn't a dead broke, deadbeat private eye. He'd lied to her. Well, that's the way it was with men. They always had something they kept from you. Just let them handle it. You didn't need to know.

Everybody lied.

She made her voice steely. "He knows you by name?"

Mitch ignored her and turned down the lane labeled *C*.

"The key said *K*10," Mae pointed out, momentarily distracted.

"I know."

"So why—"

"Because this is where Albert expects me to turn. We are breaking and entering, and I'd like Albert not to get wind of that, okay?"

Mae leaned against the car door so she could watch him better while he lied to her. "So you turn down *C* lane because that's where your shed is."

"Right." Mitch made a right turn at the end of the lane. "Watch for *K*."

"It'll be right after *J*." Mae folded her arms. "If you're so broke, why do you have an extremely expensive storage shed?"

"Mabel, we're not close enough for you to know all my secrets. Will you look for *K*, please?"

"Mitch, they're alphabetical. *K* is not going to be a surprise. And I don't know any of your secrets—"

"Good." Mitch swung right on the *K* lane.

"So this is as good a place to start learning them as any."

"This is it." Mitch cut the engine and got out, and Mae had no choice but to follow him.

A storm was blowing up, and the wind was actually cool. Mitch reached in through the car window and pulled out a blue windbreaker. "Do you want this?"

Mae shook her head and watched him as he put on the jacket, and then she followed him to the door of the shed.

He bent over the lock, trying to see the keyhole in the dim light.

She came up behind him and tried again. "Why do you—"

"Shh." Mitch turned the key and shoved the door open, fumbling for the light switch inside. When he flipped it, the shed leaped into fluorescent brightness.

It was absolutely empty.

"No." Mae's heart sank into her shoes. There was nothing there. No paintings, no furniture, no cash, not even the damn diary. "I don't believe it." She walked to the middle of the shed and turned around slowly. It was good-size, ten by twelve at least, and lined with shelves, and every inch of it was barren. When life gives you lemons, you're supposed to make lemonade, but what do you do when there aren't even any damn lemons in the place?

Mitch came in and closed the door behind him. "Don't give up yet," he said, and she ignored him. It was obviously past time for giving up. Still, when he insisted, she helped him search, looking for a slip of paper, any tiny clue that might have been left behind.

There wasn't anything.

"This makes no sense." Mae sat down where she stood at the back of the shed, her legs crossed in front of her on the concrete floor, and buried her head in her hands. "Where did it all go?"

"You mean the diary?" Mitch sat down across the shed from her, his back against the door. "That's what this is all about, right?"

Mae raised her head from her hands at the gently patronizing tone in his voice. "You haven't believed in that diary from the beginning. You're like all the rest. You say, 'Whatever you want, Mae Belle' and then you go off and do what you want. Men."

"Hey, wait a minute. I—"

"You what?" She glared at him. "You want to tell me how you're different? Well, you're not. You take checks from my Uncle Claud, and you get all macho with my Uncle Gio, and you go to mush around June and you gape at Stormy, and you lie to me and—"

"I have never lied to you." Mitch's voice was firm with conviction, but Mae had been there before.

"Oh, right. You're just a broken-down private eye, but Nick Jamieson knows you like a brother, and you rent a very expensive storage shed, and you—"

"I never said I was a broken-down private eye," Mitch observed mildly. "You just—"

"Well, what are you then?" Mae dropped her eyes from his face, knowing he was going to lie to her and hating it. Not that she expected anything else. Mitch was funny and sexy and smart and made her crazy, but he was still a—

"I'm a stockbroker," Mitch said.

Mae blinked at him across the expanse of empty shed. "You're a what?"

"My name isn't Mitchell Peatwick. It's Mitchell Kincaid, and I'm a stockbroker." Mitch sighed. "I wouldn't tell you this, but you're going to nag me until you get it out of me, anyway."

"This is true." Mae frowned, trying to stomp down the little spark of hope the word *stockbroker* had irrationally aroused in her. Stockbrokers could easily be scum, it wasn't as if he'd said he was a social worker, but she listened to him, anyway. "How did you get from stockbroker to private detective?"

"Well, I had this fantasy." Mitch made himself comfortable on the floor. "I was a good stockbroker, but after a while, it was just the same old routine. I had a couple of clients like Nick who'd give me money to risk on way-out stuff, but mostly I just made sure rich people stayed rich." He met Mae's eyes. "Rich people pay well for that sort of thing."

"I imagine so." Mae had no idea where he was going, but she didn't want to discourage him by asking.

"So a couple of years ago, I was out drinking with a friend of mine named Newton—you'd like Newton—and we were talking about what we'd always wanted to be, and I said a private detective. Like Sam Spade. A lone knight on mean streets. Saving the poor and downtrodden, especially if they had great legs. Like yours, for instance."

Mae nodded, still totally lost as to the point of the story.

"Anyway, Newton liked the idea. A lot. Then we sobered up and forgot about it, but I kept thinking about it at odd hours, and I went out about a year ago and got a P.I. license just for the hell of it. And I showed it to Newton." Mitch winced. "My first mistake. About a week later, we were at a dinner, at a tableful of associates and my boss, and we'd all been tossing back the juice, and Newton brought up my license. So I passed it around, and one of the associates, this clown named Montgomery, said something to the effect that it was typical of midlife-crisis guys to buy Porsches and day-dream about dumb new careers. Anyway, one thing led to another, and I said I could get a private investigation bureau into the black in a year." He stopped and frowned at Mae. "That's a big promise. It takes most new businesses five years to get out of the red."

"Okay," Mae said, finally seeing where this was leading. "And he bet you that you couldn't."

"Right. The rules were that I had twenty thousand as start-up capital, I couldn't use my real name to get financial business or credit and I couldn't touch any other money except what I made as a P.I. Newton volunteered to keep the books." Mitch sighed. "My boss asked who would take care of my clients, and Newton volunteered for that, too, so my boss gave me a leave of absence. I think he may have had midlife fantasies himself. And the next morning, I woke up, realized what I'd done and swore off alcohol for life. I haven't had a drink since."

"Well, that explains why you live in a tenement." Mae tilted her head at him. "How much was the bet for?"

"Ten thousand. Newton got Montgomery into another twenty thou as a side bet." Mitch shook his head. "I still can't believe he did that. Newton never takes chances with money."

"So are you going to make it?"

"Yeah, thanks to you. Your check put me over the top." Mitch smiled at her, and Mae forgot that the shed was empty and that he wasn't to be trusted and let herself fall into his smile until she had to remind herself to breathe. Things were suddenly too confusing. All the defenses she'd put up because she'd known he was hiding something were in a shambles now that he wasn't hiding anything anymore.

She tried to pull her scrambled thoughts together. "How much time did you have left? On the bet, I mean."

"The year was up Friday."

"Oh." Mae swallowed. "Close call. No wonder you took my case."

"That wasn't the only reason."

Mitch made it sound offhand, but the warmth in his voice made her swallow again. Mae tried to find her own voice, but it seemed to be quivering behind her tonsils. "What other reason?"

"I told you, I had this fantasy." Mitch tipped back his head to rest it against the door. "I dreamed that this beautiful woman came into my office and asked for my help, and she was intelligent and funny and sexy and warm and she never ever lied to me." He brought his eyes back to hers. "And then you walked in. It seemed like fate."

"Oh, no." Mae closed her eyes in guilt. "Mitch, I lied to you."

"I know," Mitch said.

Mae jerked her head up. "How do you know?"

"I guessed. Want to tell me about it?"

"Yes." Mae exhaled in relief, surprised at how much she really did want to tell him everything. She wasn't quite sure why things were different now that he'd confessed to being a stockbroker, but they were. Somehow, hearing the truth had had a liberating effect on her, and now she didn't want to play games anymore. She wanted to unload the whole mess on him so they could figure it out together, and then she'd never have to play games again. "Armand wasn't murdered. I made that up. He died in Stormy's bed, like she said." She stopped, trying to sort out the best way to explain. "I don't have any money. My parents left me the trust fund, but that evaporated. And of course, Harold and June don't have anything, either. We were all dependent on Uncle Armand. Well, actually, I could have moved out, but they—"

"I know this part," Mitch said.

"Oh, right." Mae started again. "We lived with my Uncle Armand for twenty-eight years and nothing ever changed, nothing ever left that house. And then a couple of months ago, the stuff I told you about started disappearing. That was strange enough, but then, that last Monday night, I heard him on the hall phone. He'd been on his way out the door, and the phone rang. I was in the hall upstairs, and I couldn't hear what he was saying but I could tell he was mad, so I sort of snuck up to the head of the stairs, and I heard him say, 'They can't get the money without the diary, and I've always got the diary with me.' And then he listened for a minute, and then he said, 'Look, I did everything you told me to. I've found a way out of this. You're not getting any more of my money.' And then he listened for another second or two and slammed down the receiver and stomped out, absolutely furious."

Mitch was leaning forward by this point. "Where was he going?"

Mae blinked at his obtuseness. "To the town house and Stormy, of course. Monday, Wednesday and Friday nights, just like clockwork."

"He never missed?"

"Never. Uncle Armand liked routine."

"So anyone who knew him knew that's where he'd be."

"I guess so." Mae leaned forward, too. "Look, Mitch, he wasn't murdered. I just made up that part so it would look like whoever had the diary was guilty. That way, he couldn't use it to get whatever was left of the money."

"That would only work if someone really believed Armand was murdered," Mitch told her.

"That was your job." Mae tried a small smile as an apology. "You were supposed to be stupid and go out and stir up trouble and make people believe he'd been killed. Problem was, you weren't stupid."

Mitch sighed and sat back. "The problem may be bigger than that. There's a lot of money missing here. Even if Armand died naturally in his bed, with that much money in the picture, I'd bet there's a crime somewhere. It would explain why someone's so annoyed with my work." He thought for a moment and then stood up and walked across the shed to her. "Come on, let's get out of here. Whatever was here is gone."

He held out his hand to her and she took it, letting herself enjoy its warmth and solid strength while he pulled her to her feet. She followed him to the door, relieved that she'd finally come clean, and saddened, too. She wasn't sure why she was sad, but she was fairly sure it was watching his back move away from her.

Then he reached for the light switch, and checked back over his shoulder to make sure she was right behind him before he turned out the lights, and something in the way the line of his jaw eased into the muscle in his neck hit her in the solar plexus.

No, not him, she thought, but it was a feeble thought. She'd been attracted to him that first day in the office, the way his hands had been so broad and had moved across that writing pad with such confidence, and she'd been falling for him ever since, burying it under a barrage of wiseass comments, getting to know how stubborn and exasperating and endearing and honest he was.

Getting to want him more and more.

You met him less than a week ago, she tried to tell herself, but of course, that was plenty of time for wanting somebody. A minute was plenty for wanting somebody. Now, if she'd been thinking about anything but getting him into bed—

She had a sudden vivid picture of being in bed with Mitch, his body hard against hers, his hands moving—

"Mabel, you have the damnedest look on your face. Are you all right?"

Mae swallowed. "Fine. I'm fine."

"Good." Mitch switched off the light, and in the seconds before he opened the door, Mae thought about grabbing him and pulling him down onto the floor and making him make love to her.

She was fairly sure he'd do it. And then she'd be just another librarian.

He opened the door. Lightning flashed, and the wind blew, and she shivered more in reaction to the storm than to any chill in the air.

"Here." He took off his windbreaker. "Put this on."

She started to tell him that she wasn't cold, and then she took the jacket. It was warm, and it smelled like him, and if she couldn't have him wrapped around her, she could at least have his jacket. It was pathetic, but there it was.

She put on the jacket and followed him out into the stormy dusk.

And somebody shot at them.

Mae froze, not believing that anything like that could happen outside of the movies, and Mitch grabbed her and yanked her down into the dirt, and she clung to him while another bullet whined overhead and buried itself in the shed.

SHE HAD HIM in a death grip, and Mitch was torn between holding her tight against him to keep her safe and going to find the jerk with the gun. It wasn't much of a choice, but if they just sat in the dirt beside the car until Albert noticed the shooting, they'd be dead in no time.

He had to go.

He didn't ever want to let her go, but he had to go.

"Stay here and don't move," Mitch whispered, and Mae gripped him harder for a second. Then she released him and crouched in the shadows of the huge car, nodding. "I mean it," Mitch warned her, fear for her making him stern. "Don't do that dumb stuff that women always do in the movies. You stay put."

Mae nodded again.

"Right," Mitch said in disbelief under his breath and moved silently around the back of the shed to circle toward the direction of the shots. *Why am I doing this?* he asked himself as he crept through the dim light. He wasn't even a real private detective. *Possibly because Mae Belle is watching,* he thought and then rejected the thought. Other men made fools of themselves over women, not Mitchell Peatwick Kincaid. This was stupid.

Then the shooting started again.

Mitch hit the ground and rolled into the cover of the shed on his left, only to see Mae totally exposed in her assigned place by the car. The shooter had moved. *Run, you dummy,* he screamed at her silently, and another bullet flew over her head and pinged on the car. *There's a gas tank there. He may start shooting lower. Move, damn it!*

She stayed frozen in place, and Mitch mentally called her every name in the book. Practically speaking, there was nothing he could do. If he ran out there to drag her to safety like some dumb movie hero, he'd get picked off, and then she would be in a mess. She obviously couldn't make it without him. She—

Then a bullet hit the dirt beside her, and his heart leapt up his throat, and he surged to his feet and ran past the car, yanking her to her feet and dragging her with him behind the shed.

"Why did you just sit there?" he snapped at her, shoving her behind him so she couldn't see how much he was shaking. He wanted to hold her so much, he ached with it. "You could have been killed, you dummy!"

"You told me not to move," Mae snapped back around ragged breaths. "I thought you had a plan."

"If they're actually shooting directly at you," Mitch whispered viciously, swallowing his heart back into his chest now that she was safe, "assume my plan has changed."

"*Now* you tell me." Mae peered around him into the dark lot and shuddered. "I could have been *killed.*"

"That's your fault." Mitch looked out into the darkness, too, worried at the sudden quiet. "If you had any sense . . ."

"And I knew that if I ran and got shot and was lying there, dying, bleeding into the dirt, that you would come and gather me up in your arms, and look deep into my eyes . . ."

"Shh," Mitch hissed, trying to see what was going on around him and trying not to think about gathering her up into his arms.

"And then right before I breathed my last, you'd say, '*Why did you move?*'" Mae mimicked furiously. "You make me *crazy.*"

Mitch swung around to glare at her. "I make *you* crazy? You almost got me killed. I—"

"Why isn't he shooting anymore?"

Mitch listened to the darkness. "He's probably as disgusted with you as I am." He slid his back down the shed wall until he was sitting in the gloom, glad to give his trembling knees a break. "Here's a better question. Why was he shooting at all?"

Mae slid down beside him and sagged a little against him. It took everything he had not to put his arm around her. Because then he'd kiss her. And then she'd point out that he was a cretin. And then—

Mae's voice whispered back, "Because we were in Armand's storage shed?"

"Which was empty." Mitch looked down at her drooping head. "You look beat." He craned his head back to look out into the darkness, but there was no movement anywhere.

"I am." Mae's voice sounded very far away. "Do you think he's gone?"

"Yes," Mitch said to comfort her, even though he didn't have a clue. "We'll wait a couple of minutes and go, too." Suddenly, she seemed like a little kid. An orphan. He reached out and put his arm around her, closing his eyes as he pulled her against him. "Sorry I yelled."

Mae rested her head on his shoulder. "That's okay. Sorry I didn't move."

"My fault," Mitch said, feeling magnanimous because he was so happy to be holding her. "I told you not to."

"I know." Mae's voice was faint but grumpy in the gloom. "That's why I didn't."

Mitch felt her shift softly against him, and suddenly she was Mae again, and the orphan image vanished. He squelched down the hot thoughts that swamped him and moved his arm away from her. "Are you okay?"

"No. Somebody just shot at me. I'm upset."

"Right." Mitch patted her shoulder and craned his neck for another look around. "Stay here. I'll go get the car and bring it back so you don't have to go out in the open again, and then we'll go home."

"What if you get shot?" Mae's voice was more worried than querulous.

"Then you'll have to get the car on your own." Mitch stood, losing her warmth and hating it. "Wait here. Do not move." When Mae gave a mirthless laugh, he amended that to, "Unless somebody shoots at you. In that case, run like hell."

"You bet," Mae said.

SAFE IN THE DARKNESS of the car on the way home, Mae sorted through her thoughts, trying hard to find a coherent one. She'd been under a lot of stress lately, and then there was the disappointment of the storage shed, and then getting shot at—that was bad—and now here she was, alone in the dark with Mitch, and all she could think of was that if he didn't touch her, she was going to go crazy.

And he wasn't going to touch her.

She closed her eyes so she could imagine his hands moving over her body, feel his lips against her skin, and she breathed a little deeper trying not to moan. He was a librarian addict who couldn't commit to one set of breasts. Okay, that she could deal with. What she couldn't deal with was that he wasn't interested. He'd never even made a pass. He'd never—

"You okay?"

"Yes." She turned to see him in the faint light from the dashboard. His eyes were hooded and dark and his face was craggy, and only a woman in love would have called him handsome, and she could have looked at him forever.

"We should call the police."

The police. If they got into it, Mitch would be through. The diary story would be out.

"Maybe."

Mitch glanced at her. "You don't want to tell them about the diary?"

"I don't know." Mae felt tears start. This was so dumb. She had people shooting at her and she was missing a fortune, and all she wanted to do was climb into bed with this man and make love until she lost her mind.

"Mae?"

"Can we decide in the morning? I'll be thinking better in the morning."

"Sure." His voice was deep and comforting and it set up a humming inside her like a tuning fork, and the humming moved lower and lower until she let her head drop back on the seat and just concentrated on not screaming for him.

"Do you want me to come in?" he asked when he pulled up in front of her house, and she said, *"No,"* and all but fell out of the car in her scramble to get away from him and his heat and the promise of his hands. Then Harold was there to let her in, and she pushed past him and ran up the stairs.

ON THE DRIVE BACK to his place, Mitch decided that he was going to have to stay away from Mae.

It was a bleak thought. He'd come to count on seeing her smile. He even liked watching her frown when she was annoyed or glare when she was furious. Then there was the way the sun picked out mahogany highlights in her dark hair, the way her neck curved into her shoulder, the way her calves flexed when she strode across a room, the way her laugh lighted up the whole world.

And she wasn't even a librarian.

She didn't appeal to him the way the librarians had. She wasn't shyly sexy, she was up-front, in-your-face, you-talkin'-to-me? sexy. She just stood there with her hands on her hips and dared him not to find her mind-bendingly desirable. And fascinating. And funny. And dear.

Dear? Sam Spade never found Brigid O'Shaughnessy dear. His loss.

Mitch parked illegally in front of his apartment and trudged up the stairs, thinking about how impossible it was that he should be attracted to somebody like her, somebody who would never be a good little wife, who would nag and snipe and make caustic comments....

Somebody who would meet him toe-to-toe for the rest of his life, on her own terms.

It was when he was unlocking his door that he decided he'd have to marry her. Somebody had to take care of her. And no other man would be able to stand that mouth.

The thought of marriage led to thoughts of weddings and wedding nights, and although he tried hard not to think about Mae in his bed, Mae naked in his arms, he did, anyway. The notion made him dizzy. *Maybe it's just the sex,* he told himself. *Maybe it's just more pipeline.* Then he thought about her smile and her laugh, and thought, *I'm a goner. This isn't good.*

He went into the bathroom to take a cold shower so he could get the blood back to his brain so he could figure out how to convince Mae to marry him.

Oh, and that guy who'd been shooting at them. He had to think of something to do about him, too.

He stripped off his clothes, turned the cold water on full blast and stepped under it.

MAE CRANKED OPEN the casement window in her bedroom and stuck her head out into the night. Her hair was still wet from her shower and the chill made her shiver. The air lay heavy with the recent storm, and the night wind blew cool against her white satin robe, making it move over her skin as lightning crackled a warning in the distance. Mae closed her eyes and breathed deep. She loved storms.

She loved Mitch.

She turned back into the darkened room, trying not to think about Mitch, and stepped on the polar bear rug that separated her bed from the window, scrunching her toes into the thick polyester pelt.

Armand had hated the rug. He'd wanted to get her a real polar bear pelt, and he hadn't understood when she'd said she couldn't sleep with a corpse in her room. Of course, Armand hadn't understood her room, hadn't understood why over the years she'd had the furniture taken out, the rugs removed, until now all that remained was white walls and hardwood floors, her carved pine vanity with the huge mirror that reflected back the sunlight from the windows, her oversize pine bed piled high with white down pillows and comforters, her pine worktable and bentwood chair and the polyester polar bear rug. It was all she wanted: space and light and texture. She'd thought she was going to have a home like it someday, but now it looked as if Armand had cheated her— and June and Harold—out of that, too.

She turned on the big lamp on her worktable and sat on the edge of the bed, drawing the satin sash tighter on her robe.

They weren't going to find the money. Mitch had looked everywhere, and it wasn't going to turn up. Whatever Armand had done with it, she'd never see it. It didn't matter for her. It really didn't. She'd never wanted the money, anyway. She just didn't know how she was going to take care of Harold and June on fifteen thousand a year from her job at the art institute. She wasn't sure she could feed *Bob* on fifteen thousand a year.

Maybe Mitch could invest it for her.

Mitch.

She let herself fall back into the downy thickness of the comforters and tried to distract herself with thoughts of Harold and June and Bob and the house they'd never have, but all she could think about was Mitch.

It wasn't just physical. It was the way he took care of her by not taking care of her, the way he trusted her to take care of herself. The way he made her laugh. The way she felt good just looking at him. The way she trusted him. Everybody lied, he said. She didn't believe it. In less than a week, he'd become the one person she'd trust with her life.

She thought again of the shooting, and how terrified she'd been, and how he'd been there then, and how much she'd wanted him to hold her, and how he hadn't.

I can't do this anymore.

She was dizzy with wanting him, and it was torture to spend time with him and not touch him. It had to end. The money was gone, and it was over, and she was never going to get what she wanted. She didn't know what she was going to do next, but she knew what she wasn't going to do.

She wasn't going to torment herself by seeing Mitch again.

She sat up and pulled the phone over to the edge of the table and dialed his number.

The phone rang forever, and then, just as she was about to hang up, he answered it with *"What?"*

"Mitch, this is Mae." Her voice quavered, and she swallowed to try to steady it.

"What's wrong?" He didn't sound angry anymore. "Sorry, I was in the shower. What happened? Are you all right?"

Mae took a deep breath. "You're fired."

"No, I'm not." He sounded perplexed. "What's wrong with you?"

"We're never going to find the money, and I can't afford to pay you anymore, and your week's up soon—"

"I'll work for free. I'll pick you up tomorrow and we'll talk about it."

"No!"

"Mabel, tell me what's wrong right now, or I'm coming over there."

"No!"

"Mabel—"

"All right." Mae blinked. "All right, then. But listen. Just listen." She stopped and there was nothing but silence on the other end. "All right." She swallowed. "I can't see you anymore. I'm . . . attracted to you."

Mitch's snort came over the wire like an explosion. "Well, I'm attracted to you, too, but—"

"*Just listen!*" Mae swallowed again in the silence. "I'm not just attracted to you. I want you." Once the first words were out, the others followed, uncontrollably. "I want you everywhere, every way possible. I want to touch you everywhere, I want to taste every inch of you, I want to wrap myself around you forever. I want your hands everywhere on me, and your mouth, and—" The words tumbled out of her, her voice rising, and she said things she'd never dreamed she could say to anyone, things she'd never said to herself, swinging in wilder and wilder arcs of erotic fantasy, and she said them all to him, chanted them as she got dizzier and dizzier thinking of him, until she shrieked, "And most of all, I want you hard inside me, and *I can't stand it anymore.*" Then she stopped, surprised to find herself standing, leaning against the wall by her bed, shaking from the emotion and the release and the need for him that still pounded inside her.

After a few seconds, he said, "Mae?"

She closed her eyes, feeling like a complete fool. "Yes?"

"Are you done?"

She swallowed. "Yes."

"Are you all right?"

Her breathing slowed as she thought about it. "Yes. Yes. Actually, I feel better."

"Good." His voice was preternaturally calm. "Now listen to me." He stopped for a moment, and she heard him draw a breath. "This is not a problem. Where are you?"

"I'm in my bedroom," she squeaked.

"First door at the top of the stairs, right?"

She felt her breath go and fought to get the word out. "Right."

"Good. Stay there. Don't move."

He hung up, and she heard the dial tone in her ear, and it gradually dawned on her that he was coming over.

She had promised him more than she had ever even thought of with any other man, and he was coming over. She sank slowly onto the bed, terrified and exhilarated and more aroused than she'd ever been in her whole life.

She was going to make love with Mitch.

"Oh, my God," she said and collapsed back onto the bed.

8

MITCH HUNG UP the phone, smacked his head once into the wall to get some blood back to it and headed for the door.

No, wait, he needed keys. Where were his car keys? Pants pocket. He reached for his pants on the floor and realized he was naked.

Okay, clothes first. He sat down on the bed, and it sagged under his weight, and he heard Mae's voice again in the back of his brain, reciting all the things she wanted, and he closed his eyes to keep from passing out. *Breathe*, he told himself, and he breathed in deep. *Now get dressed*.

He stood and zipped up his pants, jammed his feet into his loafers and then felt in his pocket for his keys on his way to the door. Good, they were there. He grabbed his jacket from the table and threw the door open.

Newton was standing there, one hand raised to knock. "Oh, good, you're home."

"No, I'm not." Mitch pulled on his jacket as he tried to move past him, but Newton blocked his way.

"You have to hear this." Newton's face gleamed with pride. "I've found out some astonishing things."

"Good. Good for you." Mitch tried to dodge around him.

Newton blinked at him. "What are you wearing? You look like Eurotrash. Where's your shirt?"

"*Not now*, Newton." Mitch pushed past him into the hall and ran toward the stairs.

"Wait!" Newton followed him at a more aloof shamble, losing in ground what he was gaining in dignity. "I've found out something—"

Mitch ignored him and pounded down the stairs. Exercise was good. It kept him from exploding from the thought of Mae, naked in his arms.

Then he burst through the street door and saw his car in the lights of the neon signs from the bars.

All four tires were in ribbons.

The seats were slashed down to the springs.

And every piece of glass on the car was smashed to powder. Windshields, head- and taillights, even the glass on the dash.

After an adult lifetime of firmly believing that other people can only annoy you if you let them, Mitch lost it.

His scream was still echoing down the street when Newton pushed through the apartment-house door. "You know, somebody doesn't like you," he observed, blinking at the car.

Mitch grabbed him by the jacket. "Where's your car?"

"In the garage at the end of—"

"Come on." Mitch gripped his sleeve and hauled him down the street.

"I'll drive," Newton said firmly, trying to keep up without breaking a sweat.

"The hell you will," Mitch said.

A FEW MINUTES LATER, Mae realized she was still clutching the phone and stood to hang it up. She turned and caught sight of herself in the mirror.

Her hair was in damp curls, and her face was naked. For that matter, so was she, under her robe.

Oh, great, what now? Makeup? Hair dryer? Sexy night-gown?

What sexy nightgown? She didn't own any sexy nightgowns.

Oh, great.

Mae started to pace. There was nothing to worry about. It wasn't as if this was her first time. It was just Mitch, after all.

Mitch.

She ran to the vanity and pulled a comb through her hair. Now she had damp straight hair. With a scream of frustration, she messed up her hair by scrambling her hands through it and then started to pace again, remembering all the things she'd said to him, and how she'd meant every one of them.

If he'd just get here, she could stop having a nervous breakdown from anticipation and lose her mind making love with him.

The thought made her stop pacing and close her eyes.

Hurry up, Mitch, she thought, and then she started pacing again to keep from screaming.

INTERSTATE 75 WAS still a mass of orange barrels and single-lane traffic. Of course, it would be. Summer was construction season in Ohio, and all the barrels were in bloom. Mitch was so mad he hit one on purpose.

"Try not to do that," Newton said from the passenger seat.

"It was in my way."

"Where is it exactly that we're going?"

At another time with a clearer mind, Mitch might have told him. This time, he thought about where he was going and pressed harder on the pedal. The speedometer moved from eighty to ninety.

"This is one-lane," Newton observed.

A car loomed up ahead, growing larger instantaneously. Newton moaned, and Mitch hit the brake, screaming down to thirty before they came up behind it, bumper to bumper.

"The hell with this." Mitch swung out onto the berm to pass him.

Behind them, a siren wailed.

FIFTEEN MINUTES LATER, Mae was climbing the walls.

Where was he? A plethora of ideas crowded her mind: he'd met somebody else, he'd stopped for a sandwich, he'd had a new idea about where to look for the money, he'd changed his mind about making love to her, he'd stopped for condoms—

She stopped pacing. Condoms. What if he didn't have any? She didn't have any. Oh, great. Maybe Harold and June—no. Birth control was no longer a problem for Harold and June. She needed somebody young. She thought about making an emergency call to Stormy, and then it hit her.

There had been condoms in the box from Armand's town house.

She flew down the hall to his room and rummaged in the box to grab a handful of the red foil packages. Then she ran back to her room and yanked open the worktable drawer and threw them inside.

Then she sat down on the bed again and tried to stop breathing like a draft horse.

Now all she needed was Mitch.

Where *was* he?

MITCH PUT THE TICKET in the breast pocket of his jacket and noticed for the first time that he wasn't wearing a shirt.

He was out of control.

"I'm sorry, Newton."

"I'm sure you have your reasons."

"I do." Mitch took a deep breath. "But I can't act like this." He thought about Mae again, and his head swam a little. It would not be good for him to go screaming into her bedroom. Think Cary Grant.

"I know where some of the money went," Newton said.

Mitch came back from Mae's bedroom. "What?"

"The money. I know what happened to one and a half million of it."

Mitch focused on Newton completely for the first time since Mae's phone call. "What?"

"He gave it to Stormy."

"What?"

Newton nodded. "He bought her a condo—"

"That I knew."

"For five hundred thousand."

Mitch turned the key and eased the car back onto the highway. "So where's the other million?"

"Swiss bank account. His idea."

Mitch turned to him, startled. "How the *hell* did you find that out?"

"She told me."

"She . . ." Words failed him.

"At lunch. Today." Newton checked his watch. "I'm picking her up for dinner in a half hour. Where are we going? I don't want to be late."

"Mae's." Mitch's voice was faint because he was stunned. "You're dating Stormy?"

"Yes. Why are we going to Mae's?"

"She called me." Mitch felt the heat rise again. No. He was going to be calm. Just like Cary Grant.

He thought of Mae's smile, and Mae's laugh, and then he thought of Mae's body and gripped the wheel tighter.

"Is she in trouble?" Newton asked, alarmed.

"No. She just wanted me to come over."

"Then why are we rushing like this?"

Mitch met his eyes. "Because she wanted me. To come over. Now." He looked back at the road.

Newton frowned at him for a moment. "I don't... Oh." His forehead cleared and he turned to look out the back window. "Step on it. I'll watch for the police."

MAE WAS LYING crosswise on her bed staring at the ceiling when she heard a car pull up in front. It didn't sound like the Catalina. For one thing, it had a working muffler. Great, she was getting company, and it wasn't Mitch.

It was so unfair. Other women got great love scenes. She got the Keystone Kops.

Then she heard someone pounding up the stairs, and there was a quick rap on the door, and then Mitch was in the room with her.

She sat up as if she'd been catapulted and slid to her feet, stunned to see him there in the flesh. She blinked. Really in the flesh. He didn't have a shirt on under his jacket.

He closed the door behind him and stood looking at her. "Hi."

Mae blinked at him again. "Hi."

His eyes traveled down her body, and she smoothed her satin robe nervously. "You look really nice," he said.

She swallowed hard. "Thank you."

He closed his eyes. "Mae, if you've changed your mind, just tell me now so I can go kill myself."

Relief washed over her and she laughed, the sound bubbling up from inside her, and she felt her whole body soften with her laughter, and all her need for him came back. "If you don't make love to me, I'll die," she said, and he came toward her, shaking his head and laughing at himself as he stripped off his jacket and dropped it on the floor.

"You don't know how long I've wanted you," he said as he slid his arms around her, and she shuddered as his body touched her.

"Kiss me," she said, and he did, and every fear and doubt she had evaporated as his mouth touched hers, supple and hot and intoxicating. She opened her lips to taste him, and he touched her tongue with his as she slumped against him, her hands gripping the corded muscles in his back while the heat in her rose and made her dizzy. Then he was pulling her toward the bed, and she undid the belt to her robe and let it fall open. He closed his eyes when he saw her, sliding his hands under her robe, up her sides to cup her breasts, and she dug her fingernails into his shoulders to stop herself from moaning with pleasure. He pulled her onto the bed on top of him, rolling until she was under him, and moved his mouth to her breast, and then she did moan, lacing her fingers in his hair to pull him closer. His lips moved up to the pulse of her throat, and then to her mouth, and she swelled under him like a wave, stroking her hands up his back, tasting every inch of him with her fingertips.

"Oh, God, Mae, I have wanted you," he murmured to her, and she opened her eyes to see him gazing down on her, his eyes black with desire. And when he bent to kiss her again, she stopped him, her hands cupping his face.

"Let me look at you," she whispered. "I can't believe it's you. I can't believe it's us."

"I wanted you from the first moment I saw you. From the first minute you came in my door." He smiled at her. "In that damn pink suit." He closed his eyes and put his forehead on hers. "I can't believe it's us, either."

"Make love to me," Mae whispered. "Make love to me all night."

"Whatever you want," Mitch whispered back. "Whatever you want, Mae. I swear."

He kissed her then, a long deep kiss that went into her spine and made her body curve around his, fitting against him, and his hands moved, too, molding her to him. "What do you want?" he whispered in her ear, and his breath made her body tighten and arch. "Whatever you want, you can have."

She ran her fingers through his hair and pushed his head down to her breast, gasping a little when his tongue caressed and teased her nipple and then moaning when he took her breast in his mouth and sucked hard. She could feel the pull in her groin and arched up under him, and outside, the thunder rolled in the distance, and the wind blew the curtains back away from the window she'd forgotten to close. He moved to her other breast, dropping kisses into her cleavage, and then she felt his tongue on her again as his hand came up to stroke the dampened breast he'd abandoned. Mae gave up any pretense of sanity and just lost herself in the touch of his hand and his mouth and the heat that was everywhere. She arched up again, and then she wrapped her fingers in his hair and pushed his head lower.

She felt the weight of his head on her stomach, his hands stroking down her sides to her hips, and then he licked inside her. Her hips spasmed, and he trapped her there, his hands imprisoning her against his mouth. Outside, the storm began in earnest, blowing the cold storm breeze through the open window and across her burning body, and her skin tightened under the double onslaught of the wind and his mouth. She grabbed blindly behind her to clutch at the pine headboard as he slowly, rhythmically, inexorably stroked his tongue inside her, probing and sucking and driving her out of her mind. Her moans were drowned in the thunder, and all she knew was the heat of his mouth pressed against her and the chill, rain-thick air tightening her body. Then she lost even that in the pressure that welled up inside her, making her twist against him, and then it all exploded, and her body jerked over and over again as she sobbed in her release.

Then he was kissing his way back up to her, nibbling and biting her sweat-dampened flesh, and she wrapped her legs around him, feeling his muscled thighs between her soft ones. "I want you inside me," she said through her clenched teeth, still shuddering with the aftershocks of her climax. "I want you inside me *now!*" and he said, "Wait. I want you, too. Wait." He kissed her, his mouth hot on hers, and she thought that she could spend the rest of her life in that kiss if she had to. Then he finished fumbling with the condom and pulled her to him, and then he was inside her. She writhed at the intoxicating shock of him filling her, and outside, the thunder crashed again, and the lights went out.

The lightning flashed into the room like a strobe light. She looked up into his craggy face, and her blood boiled with the fact that it was him, that it was them together, part of the storm. He rocked into her once and moaned into her neck, and then he rolled so that she was on top, and he was hard against her, and she lost her place in reality for a moment because he felt so good. The roll brought them too close to the edge, and they slid off the bed, still joined, on the thick comforter. The impact of their landing thrust them closer together, and Mae gasped, and Mitch held her tighter and said, "Are you all right?" and she breathed, "Don't *ever* stop."

She flexed her hips to roll them away from the tangle of the comforter and found herself on top of him again, on the rug, and Mitch started when he saw the open jaws of the bear next to his head. "It's polyester," she said, laughing softly in his ear, drunk with lust and love and the storm. Then she pushed herself up, straddling him, and he stroked his hands roughly across her breasts. The rain lashed at them both, cold rain on hot skin, and she rocked against him until he closed his eyes and drew in a deep ragged breath. She felt it start again deep inside her, the tightening and fire and the crackle in her veins, and she stopped, clenching herself down on him. His hands gripped her hips and pulled her tight against him, and she gave herself over to him and felt everything in her body rise and explode and crash with the thunder as the spasms came again and again until she fell sated against his chest.

They lay there on the rug, trying to breathe, clutching each other as rain fell on them through the open window, and then Mitch kissed her forehead, and whispered, "Mabel, it's raining," and she smiled, and let him roll and pull her to her feet and lead her back to the bed. And when they were wrapped in the comforter and in each other's arms again, listening to the pounding of the storm, Mitch gently smoothed back her wet hair and said, "Thank you for calling me. I damn near killed myself to get here, but you were worth it."

Mae laughed into his neck. "Thank you for coming."

Mitch laughed, too. "Anytime."

She tightened her arms around him. "I never knew anything could feel as good as holding you." When he didn't answer, she pulled back to look up at him from the dim light of the window. "Mitch?"

"I'm here." He traced the line of her face with his fingers, smoothing them across her lips, and then bent to kiss her before he whispered, "I'm amazed at us, but I'm here." He held her tighter. "This is so good it's scary."

"Then don't think about it." Mae snuggled back against him.

"I don't want to think about anything else," he said into her hair.

She held him, listening to the beat of his heart and the patter of the fading storm, and they were both almost asleep when the lights came back on.

Mitch jerked awake, and Mae patted his chest. "I'll get it." She rolled away only to feel his hand move down her back, his fingers playing over the bumps of her vertebrae. "Don't." He pulled her back against him, his breath warm against the back of her neck. "I like looking at you naked."

Mae snuggled back against him, her rear end curving into his hips. "I don't know. You know what this sort of thing leads to." She captured his hand and brought it to her breast.

"Your problem is you're shy." Mitch nibbled on her neck and made her shudder with pleasure. "Good thing I'm an optimist and brought spare condoms."

"Hey, I'm prepared, too," Mae said, pulling away in mock indignation only to fall back against him when his hand recaptured her breast. She stretched and yanked open the drawer and handed him one of Armand's foil-wrapped packages. "So there."

Mitch took it and made a move to toss it back on the table, but then he stopped, moving his other hand off her body and rolling away from her.

"Mitch?" Mae sat up. He was staring at the package, holding it up to the light.

"Lie back a minute, will you?" He pressed her gently onto the pillows, bending over her to stare at the package as he held it to the lamp. Then he looked down at her. "Mabel, you don't have a biological clock you forgot to tell me about, do you?"

She struggled to sit up. "What are you talking about? I'm thirty-four." He was watching her naked struggle with interest, and she stopped. "What are you looking at?"

"You're a very distracting woman. And we're definitely going to make love again, but not with this condom. It has a hole in it."

"What?" Mae sat up, grabbing the sheet at the last minute and holding it over her. "Give me that."

Mitch held it out of her reach. "Let go of the sheet first."

Mae tried to look stern. "Let me see that condom."

Mitch shook his head. "The sheet first."

She lunged for the condom, and he yanked on the sheet, and they both fell over, intertwined, Mae laughing in spite of herself.

Mitch licked his tongue over her breast. "You know, arguing with you is going to be a lot more fun from now on."

Mae shoved his head away and held the condom up to the lamp. Dead in the center was a tiny pinpoint of light. "You're right." She dropped the condom, rolling to open the drawer.

"I'm always right." Mitch trailed his hand lazily up her thigh as she stretched to gather up the other condoms. "You know, you really do have a world-class ass."

"Thank you." Mae rolled back over and dropped the condoms on the bed, picking up one and holding it to the light. Another hole, dead center. "How did you notice this?"

"You can feel the hole in the foil." Mitch picked up one of the other packages and held it to the light. "This one, too."

"They all have holes." Mae slumped back against the pillows.

"I'd complain to your druggist." Mitch scooped up the last of the packets and leaned over Mae to toss them on the table. Since he was there, he bent to kiss her on the neck.

"They were Armand's."

Mitch jerked his head back. "What?"

"They were in the box we found the key in. There were dozens of them, remember?"

Mitch hesitated and then nudged her hip with his. "Come on. Let's go look at the rest of them."

"Now?" Mae said, but he was already bending over her, reaching for his pants.

EVERY CONDOM in the box had a hole in it.

"What good would it do for Armand to get Stormy pregnant?" Mae asked Mitch where he sat next to her on the floor of Armand's bedroom.

"It could be Stormy poking holes, you know." Mitch tossed the last condom back in the box. "Maybe she thought she'd trump Barbara if she had a baby."

"No." Mae's voice was positive. "Armand didn't like kids. The only reason he kept me was to . . ." Her voice trailed off.

"To keep June," Mitch finished. "Would Armand knock Stormy up to keep her from leaving when he married Barbara?"

"Well, it's low enough for him." Mae sounded doubtful. "I just don't see Armand poking holes in condoms."

"Looks like I need to read another diary. What else is in here that we missed?" Mitch stirred his hand through the items in the box.

Mae yawned. "Mitch, it's the middle of the night. Can we do this in the morning?"

"No. We're going to be too busy making love in the morning." He held up a handful of lip balm sticks. "Your uncle had a bad Chap Stick habit, didn't he?"

"So this is how it ends," Mae said sadly. "One minute making love like crazed animals, the next minute discussing Chap Stick."

Mitch shoved the box away. "I'm a professional, ma'am. My professional instincts have been aroused."

Mae blinked at him, trying hard to look sad and vulnerable. "I liked it better when your other instincts were aroused."

"Fine." Mitch grabbed the back of her robe and yanked her to the floor, rolling on top of her.

"This is good." Mae bit him on the neck.

"No, it isn't." Mitch winced away from her teeth. "The only condoms we have without holes are back in your room." He kissed her once, hard, and then let it melt into a longer, softer, tongue-tangled kiss.

When she spoke again, Mae's voice was a lust-drunken murmur. "Let's go back to my room."

"Whatever you want, Mabel," Mitch said. "Whatever you want."

MITCH WOKE UP the next morning the way he always did: badly. First he struggled to consciousness through the heavy drug of his natural sleep, then he squinted and frowned against the sunlight that filled the room, then he hauled his mind over to the problem of why there was so damn much light in his apartment, then he dealt with the idea that he wasn't in his apartment and then finally, he absorbed the mind-bending fact that Mae's warm, lush body was curved naked against him.

Then he remembered everything, and for the first time in his entire life, Mitch was delighted to be awake. He stretched slowly, trying not to wake Mae, feeling his muscles faintly ache from the athletics of the night before, shivering at the slide of her skin against his. Then he pulled her close to feel her softness squash against him even though he knew it would wake her up.

He wanted her awake, anyway.

She stretched against him, and he enjoyed it, and then she moved her head higher on his shoulder and sighed into his ear, and he enjoyed that, and then her hand trailed down his chest, and he almost passed out from pleasure.

"Good morning," she murmured, and licked her tongue into his ear, and he said, "Mabel, you have no idea how good a morning it's going to be," and pinned her under him.

Then the screaming and shouting started downstairs.

Mitch vaulted out of bed and headed to the door, only to stop when Mae grabbed for him and said, "*Wait.* You're naked."

"Right." He fumbled for his pants, only momentarily distracted when she flitted by him as she slid on her robe, and then she was looking out the door to see what the shouting was about.

"Stop it," she called down, and there was silence. "Carlo, you sit down until I can get some clothes on. I mean it. Stop it." She slammed the door without waiting for an answer. "You've got to get out of here," she said to Mitch.

Mitch scowled at her. "I am not running away from Carlo."

Mae put her hands on her hips, and Mitch closed his eyes, trying not to think about what great hips she had. "It's not running away, it's saving me from a hassle. I don't want to referee any fight right now. I've got enough troubles." Her eyes went past him, and she froze. "Oh, *no!*"

"What?" Mitch wheeled around, but all he saw was the worktable with the lamp and Mae's clock.

"I'm late for work." She ran to her closet and started pulling out clothes. "And I need a shower, and I'm not going to get one because I have to take care of Carlo first . . . oh, hell!"

Mitch put his arms around her and held her close. "Tell work you're not coming in, and tell Carlo to get lost, and I'll spend the rest of the day with you in the shower." She slumped against him, tightening her arms around his waist, and he took a deep breath to keep from passing out from happiness.

"I can't," she said into his chest, and the tickle from her breath made him dizzy. "But it's a great offer, and I'm going to remember it." She pulled away from him. "Just wait here until I get rid of him."

The pounding on the door jolted both of them. "Mae? Mae, who's in there with you?"

"That's it." Mitch started for the door and Carlo.

"No," Mae whispered and hauled him back. "No. I can't handle this if you're here."

He sighed and said, "All right. But only for you would I do this." He shoved his feet into his loafers and picked up his jacket. "You got any cab fare?"

"I gave you every cent I had last night." She picked up her car keys from the table and tossed them to him. "Take the Mercedes. I'll get money from June and take a cab."

"When do you get off?" Mitch pocketed the keys. "I'll pick you up."

The pounding accelerated.

"Five." Mae shot an anxious glance at the door. "Carlo, knock it off," she called. "I'm getting dressed."

The pounding stopped, and Mitch rolled his eyes and moved toward the window.

"What are you doing?"

Mitch threw one leg over the sill and grinned back at her. "There is no end to my talents."

"You'll get killed!" She grabbed his arm, but he kissed her, enjoying her mouth as if it were the first time, and then he pried her fingers off.

"There's a trellis." He found it with his foot and pulled his other leg through the window. "See? Piece of cake." He climbed down, and when he was on the ground, he looked up and saw her framed in the window, the morning breeze tossing her curls. She was smiling down at him, and her face was like the sun, and he stood there, rapt, amazed all over again that they were together, and that she was smiling at him.

"What's wrong?" she called down softly.

Mitch had always thought that "It is the east, and Juliet is the sun," was the dumbest pick-up line he'd ever heard, but it suddenly made sense. "I just figured out why Romeo killed himself."

Mae's smile widened. "Well, don't do it, even if you see my corpse. It'll be a trick. I'm staying alive just to drive you crazy."

"Thank you," Mitch said fervently.

Mae jerked her head around to look back into the room. "I've got to go. Get out of here. I'll see you tonight."

"Count on it," Mitch said, and then she was gone, and the day seemed a little dimmer, and he turned dizzily toward the back of the house and Mae's Mercedes.

MAE OPENED the door and glared as Carlo came stomping into the room. "Listen to me. This stops now. I've had it with you. You can stop following me around, and threatening my dates, and acting like you own me. We're cousins. That's all we're going to be. Ever." She stopped because the misery on Carlo's face was overwhelming. "I'm sorry, Carlo, but it's never going to be anything else. I grew up with you. You're like my brother."

"It's that Peatwick guy, isn't it?"

"No. I'd feel like this even without the Peatwick guy." Mae put her arm around him and kissed him on the cheek. "It's us. I don't feel that way about you, and I never will. And you don't feel that way about me, either. You just think you should, so you go around acting all proprietary."

"I love you," Carlo protested.

"Then why have you slept with everything that moved and said yes since puberty?"

"If that's all this is about," Carlo began.

"No, that's not what this is about." Mae fought back her exasperation. "People who are in love do not sleep with other people they're not in love with." Carlo opened his mouth to protest, and she held up her hand to stop him. "I know, I know, you were saving me for marriage, but Carlo, I wasn't saving me for marriage, why should you? You just got this idea in your mind. Well, it's time to let go of it."

"No," Carlo said, and before Mae could start again, June knocked on the door and opened it.

"I'm sorry," she said, looking terrified. "But the police are here."

MAE FOLLOWED Carlo downstairs, still wrapped in her white satin robe, trying to remember when she'd had a twenty-four hours like her last one.

"Mae Belle Sullivan?" one of the officers said when she reached the bottom step.

"Yes." She took a step back.

"You're—"

"Back off," Carlo snarled.

"Hey." The other cop stared at him. "You're Carlo Donatello."

Carlo glared back. "So?"

"So you're under arrest. There's a warrant out for you. Malicious destruction on some guy's car."

"Oh, no." Mae sank onto the step.

"They lifted your prints, pretty boy," the cop said cheerfully. "You're screwed. You also have the right to remain silent—"

"What about her?" The other officer jerked his head at Mae.

"Wait a minute." Carlo turned back to her, and Mae stood up.

"I'll call Uncle Gio," she began, but he put his arms around her. She tried to pull away, and then he whispered in her ear, "They're here for you, too. Get out of here."

She blinked up at him, and then he said aloud, "I'll call Grandpa from the station. You go upstairs and get dressed," and she nodded and turned to stumble blindly up the stairs.

"Wait a minute," one of the cops called after her, and the last thing she heard was Carlo growling, "Let her get dressed."

She closed the door behind her and immediately moved to the closet, yanking out the first dress her hand touched. She dropped her robe to the floor and pulled the pink flowered dress over her head, trying to think as she moved but not having much success. Nothing made sense. She grabbed underwear out of the drawer and crammed it in her purse, and then she went to the window.

If Mitch could do it, she could, too.

A minute later, she was running across the backyard of the mansion to the street that ran behind it.

She had no idea where she was going, she just knew it was away.

MITCH PULLED UP in front of his office feeling like the king of the world. He was showered, shaved and dressed, he was driving a Mercedes and he was going to marry the most amazing woman he'd ever met.

It occurred to him in the elevator that he hadn't mentioned marriage the night before, and made a mental note to propose the next time he saw her. He was pretty sure it was going to be a formality. Judging by the previous night, *no* was not a word Mae was familiar with.

So he was feeling pretty chipper when he got to his office and began to tackle the work that had backed up in the week he'd been dealing with Mae. He sorted through the mail, tossing the ads and the catalogs, and then, as he slit open the first envelope, he punched the button on his answering machine.

There were seven messages, and every one of them was a client firing him.

By the time he'd listened to the last one, Mitch had given up any pretense of reading his mail. He pulled the phone toward him and dialed the number of the last client on the machine. "Mr. Belden? This is Mitch Peatwick," he began, only to hear a dial tone in his ear. He got hang-ups on the next three calls, but the fifth one finally gave him a clue. "I don't know what the hell you did, Peatwick," the guy said, "but it was dumb. Good luck." Then he hung up, too.

Mitch pushed the phone away, no longer interested in talking to ex-clients. Someone had obviously gotten to them. It didn't take a rocket scientist to narrow down the list of who that might be.

He was getting one hell of a set of in-laws.

The only question left was, why? Aside from pure cussedness, there was no reason for them to want to put him out of business. Unless he was getting close to something someone didn't want him to know about. Like the diary.

A rap on the office door broke him out of his reverie. "What?" he said, and his dried-up little landlord came in. Mitch scowled at him. "The rent is paid, Mr. Richardson, and I'm having a bad day. Go away."

"It's gonna get worse," Richardson rasped. "You're evicted."

"I'm what?"

"Evicted." Richardson put a check on the desk. "There's your rent back. Get out of here."

Mitch sat back and stared at him until the man broke a sweat. "Why?" he asked.

"New owner." Richardson edged his way to the door. "Doesn't like P.I.s. Says they bring down the tone of the place."

"This place has no tone." Mitch stood. "Who's the new owner?"

"I don't know, and I don't care. You're evicted." Richardson had managed to sidle his way through the door by now, and he reached out and slammed it behind him.

Mitch sat back down in his chair.

None of it made sense.

And it wasn't going to as long as he sat there.

He grabbed his jacket, ran downstairs and pointed the Mercedes toward the art museum and Mae, stopping at an ATM only long enough to pick up cash to pay her back for the gas money the night before. He was just getting back in the car, when the police pulled up.

There were two of them, one tall and female and the other short and male, and they didn't look amused to see him.

"Is this your car?" The male cop looked up at him, seemingly annoyed about having to look up at him.

"No, it belongs to a friend of mine," Mitch said. "Do not tell me it's been reported stolen."

"Nope." The woman officer took a notebook out of her breast pocket. "What's your friend's name?"

Mitch shifted his eyes from one to the other. "Mae Belle Sullivan. What's going on here?"

"You wouldn't happen to know where she is, would you?" the male officer asked.

"Yes," Mitch said with exaggerated patience. "She's at the Riverbend Art Institute. She works there."

"Nope." The woman moved her head once to the right and once to the left, conserving her strength. "We checked. She's not there. When was the last time you saw her?"

"This morning." Mitch scowled at both of them. "What the hell is this about?"

"She's wanted for murder," the male cop said. "We'd like you to come downtown with us."

"Just a few questions," the policewoman said.

"I want my lawyer," Mitch said.

9

NICK WAS JOVIAL when he joined Mitch in the interrogation room. "What did you do now, Sundance? Sell Bolivian tin mines to somebody besides me?"

"It's not me," Mitch said, and Nick's smile faded at his tone. "They want Mae for murder."

Nick blinked. "Whose murder?"

"On a guess, Armand's. He's the only body in the picture at the moment." Mitch got up and started to pace. "There's something going on here, Nick. I thought Armand was doing it, looting his own estate, but now there's other stuff coming down." He stopped pacing. "There's no chance that Armand is still alive, is there? I mean, people did see the body?"

"Tess heard that the university med school got the remains," Nick pointed out. "And somebody signed a death certificate."

"Somebody could have been bought off."

Nick sat down. "Let's take this from the top. Exactly whom am I representing, you or Mae?"

"Well, preferably both, but if you have to choose, choose Mae. I'm just in here for driving her car and not knowing where she is."

"You really don't know?"

Mitch held up his hand. "Scout's honor. The last I saw of her was this morning. She didn't mention anything about going on the lam later."

"If you don't know, tell them you don't know."

"I did. They didn't seem to find it convincing."

Nick pushed back his chair. "Let me see what I can do, but then you and I are going to have a long talk."

"No problem." Mitch slumped back in his chair. "All my clients fired me this morning, and my landlord evicted me from my office. I'm pretty much free."

"One problem at a time," Nick said and left to spring Mitch.

AN HOUR LATER, Mitch stood outside the police station, wilting under the blast of the noon sun and figuring out his next move.

Nick came out to join him and jerked his head toward the Mercedes. "Get in."

Once inside with the air conditioner on, he turned to Mitch. "This isn't good. The police got an anonymous tip Saturday afternoon that Armand had been poisoned. Then this morning they got a page from his diary in the mail that implies that somebody was putting the squeeze on him to put money in Mae's trust fund. That somebody is logically Mae."

Mitch relaxed. "That can't be right. She doesn't have any money."

"She didn't have until a couple of weeks ago." Nick looked unhappy. "According to bank statements, during the past fourteen weeks, right up to his death, Armand deposited almost eight million dollars to her trust fund account."

Mitch blinked. "How many?"

Nick smiled grimly. "Eight big ones. One deposit alone was for six million. She's got a motive, Mitch."

Mitch swallowed. "Nick, everybody in Riverbend had a motive to kill Armand. She'd have to get in line."

"She also had means. The police got a warrant and went to the house this morning and found Armand's pill bottle in his room. Mae's prints are all over the bottle."

"Big deal. So are mine. We both handled it last night."
Mitch frowned. "How the hell did they get Mae's prints?"

"They took them from her room."

"And while they were doing that, she skipped?"

"No, she skipped while they were arresting Carlo. For vandalizing your car."

Mitch started. "I didn't call in a police report on that yet."

"Newton did it for you last night. He told the police it was probably Carlo. The Riverbend PD is very enthusiastic about Carlo. That bit with the finger really annoyed them, and then they showed up at Mae's with the warrant and got him as a bonus. They're pretty pleased in general."

Mitch put his head on the steering wheel. "So now Carlo thinks I turned him in. Great. The last time he thought somebody ratted on him, Armand died. Thank you, Newton."

"Forget Carlo. Think Mae. As soon as you find her, bring her in."

"I don't know where—"

"Don't mess with me on this, Mitch." Nick looked grim. "As soon as you find her, bring her to me, and I will go with her to the police. This fugitive bit is not good. We've got to get her off the street."

"I don't want her to have an arrest record."

"I may be able to stall them on that." Nick shifted in his seat. "They've got enough to charge her, but I don't think they're happy about it. They're not dumb, these guys. If I can guarantee she'll stay put, they may release her to me. But she's got to come in. If they find her, they'll arrest her, and all I'll be able to do is mop up."

"And get her off," Mitch prompted.

"That, too, but let's hope to hell it never gets to court. Mae's awfully photogenic. She could be the *Hard Copy* flavor-of-the-month."

"Oh, hell."

"Forget that for now. Just find her." Nick started to get out of the car. "Oh, I forgot. What do you want me to do about the eviction?"

"Find out who's evicting me, for starters. But I have a pretty good idea whose behind it."

Nick nodded. "Sure. I'll get somebody on it. Wrongful eviction. Financial harassment. I'll make something up. Anything else while I'm at it? Paternity suit? Breach of promise? Prenuptial?"

"Nah. Mae can have anything I've got."

Nick grinned. "You and Mae, huh?"

"You don't sound very surprised."

"I'm a lawyer. Nothing surprises me."

Mitch shook his head. "Nothing used to surprise me until I met Mae. Now everything does."

Nick's expression sobered. "Find her, Mitch."

Mitch nodded. "That's my plan."

MAE HAD WALKED for an hour before she realized where she was going.

She stopped and looked at the tree-lined, brick-paved street. Armand's town house was just around the corner.

Where would the police look for her first? Gio's or Claud's, probably. Work, definitely. Mitch's, maybe.

And sooner or later, Armand's place. But probably later.

She turned the corner and walked to Armand's front door, fumbling in her purse for the key so she could unlock the door and get inside as swiftly as possible. But once inside the cool dimness of the hall, she stood trembling, finally reacting to the shock of the police. "They're here for you," Carlo had said, and she'd accepted it at once. Carlo knew about police. If he said they'd come for her, they had.

And it could only be for one thing. Somebody was finally taking her lie about Armand's death seriously.

She moved slowly through the archway into the living room, listening to see if anyone else was in the house. It seemed filled with the empty silence that only deserted places have, a desolation born of loss. People had been happy here once, and now it was empty. She could feel the unhappiness in her groin, like a cramp, and she ached for Stormy and what she had lost. Even though Armand had been a jerk, Stormy had still loved him, and in his own way, he'd loved her. And love was a terrible thing to lose.

She knew that because now she had love to lose. She had Mitch.

She sank onto the soft amber couch and tried to think.

She couldn't stay here too long. Sooner or later, they'd come here, if only to look for clues. The temptation to go upstairs and crawl into a bed and never come out again was overwhelming. She could live there forever, going out into the garden at night to see the stars. It would be a sanctuary, and she could stay there alone forever and no one would hurt her.

Except that someone had to take care of June and Harold, and the police would definitely show up sooner or later, and there were no sanctuaries. There were no safe places in life. That's why you had to keep moving.

And besides, she didn't want to be alone. She wanted to be with Mitch.

Think, she told herself, but she didn't know enough to puzzle out what was happening to her. Something had happened to all that money, but she didn't know what. Someone was shooting at her, but she didn't know who. The police wanted her, but she didn't know why. She thought longingly of Mitch, not as a savior because he wasn't the savior type, but as a partner, somebody to share the puzzle with. She

wanted to tell him everything and say, "What do you think?"
and argue the possibilities with him, go and find out things
with him, and just be with him. Not for comfort, not for
support, just for the rightness of being with him.

But he wasn't there, and she was alone, and she had to
think of something fast. She let herself fall back against the
couch and rest for just a minute. She was so tired from no
sleep the night before and the adrenaline rush that morning
and the six-mile walk in a daze that thinking became as
strenuous as lifting heavy weights. She was so very tired. She
closed her eyes, and tried hard to think, and tried very hard
not to panic.

"OH, THANK GOD, Mitch!" June dragged him through the
front door and threw her arms around him. "She's gone, and
the police were here!"

Mitch patted her on the back. "Get a grip, kid. Are you
okay?"

"No." June sniffed. "I don't know where she is. And Harold's eye is swelled shut."

Mitch blinked at her. "What does Harold's eye have to do
with this?"

"Carlo hit him this morning when Harold tried to stop him
from going up to Mae's room." June sniffed again, her expression a hybrid of anger and sorrow. "We're trying to decide what to do."

"Let me see this eye." Mitch prodded her toward the back
of the house. "And then I'll take care of the rest."

"Oh, good." June's shoulders sagged with relief as she led
him toward the kitchen, her usual glide degenerating into
more of a totter. "I knew you were going to be good for us
when Mae brought you home the first time."

Us? Up until then, Mitch's plans for commitment had centered on Mae, but June's assumption brought him up to date.

Mae meant June and Harold, too. And Bob. He watched June's platinum head bob in front of him as she shoved open the kitchen door, and felt a rush of affection for her. She wasn't particularly deep or intelligent, and God knew, Harold wasn't anybody's grandpa, but they'd loved Mae and brought her up to be the woman he couldn't leave, and he owed them. They were good people.

Harold looked up as they came in, his eye purple and swelled completely shut, and Mitch felt rage tighten his throat.

"Carlo needs smacking," he said to Harold.

"I tried." Harold's face fell into morose pleats. "He's a fast son of a bitch."

"Then I'll have to hit him from behind." Mitch bent to get a better look at Harold's eye. "How's your head feel?"

"I'm okay."

"Stop being a hero." Mitch gently lifted the swollen lid back and checked Harold's pupil. "Headache?"

"Yeah." Harold's good eye shifted to June. "It's not bad."

"Dizziness?"

"No." For the first time since they'd met, Harold looked at Mitch without glaring at him. "It's not a concussion. It's just one hell of a bad black eye."

"Okay." Mitch straightened. "I have to find Mae. Are you two going to be okay on your own for a while?"

June swallowed, but Harold said, "Hell, yes."

"Stay here," Mitch told him. "I have no idea when I'll be back, but if Mae's in a mess and I need to reach you, I want you here."

Harold nodded. "Right."

"Do you know where she might have gone?"

Harold shook his head and winced. "I don't even know how she got out of her room."

Mitch grinned. "She climbed down the trellis. I'm her role model."

"That's probably why she's in this mess now," Harold said, but his voice held no venom. "Go find her."

"Please," June quavered.

Mitch patted her shoulder. "I've got this all under control. Don't worry about a thing. Just keep ice on that eye."

On an impulse, he stopped in the library and picked up the 1952 diary, and then he walked back out into the heat and stood looking at the Mercedes Mae hated and thought, *What the hell do I do now?*

MAE STARTED out of her reverie when the postman shoved the mail through the slot. She moved silently to the front door to see who was there, and then relaxed when she saw the stack of junk mail on the carpet. She picked up the mail and sorted through it, but there was nothing personal, nothing that every other resident on the block wasn't getting, too: catalogs for bedding and fashion and toys, sale reminders, coupon fliers. She dropped the mail on the table and went upstairs, trailing her fingers over the railing as she went.

It would be nice to have a little place with a bedroom at the top of a flight of curving stairs. A bedroom with a big, warm, soft bed. A big soft bed with Mitch in it and the rest of the world gone away.

Mae closed her eyes at the thought, craving sleep because she craved oblivion.

She tried the first door on the right at the top of the stairs.

It was a guest bedroom, but there was something odd about it. Mae stood inside the door and frowned, trying to put her finger on what was wrong. The walls were painted bright yellow and trimmed with a yellow flowered border, and all the furniture was white with yellow flowers and butterflies painted on it, and it was very pretty but not quite like the rest of the house, somehow. And in the middle of the room was a plain single bedstead with nothing pretty or comfortable about it. It looked temporary.

Maybe Stormy had ordered a bed that went better, but it hadn't arrived yet. Mae tried to mentally delete the bed from the room. It definitely didn't belong. What would? Mae tried to picture a white bedstead with the butterflies and flowers, covered with a flowered comforter. Or a quilt. It was the kind of room she would have loved to have as a child.

Mae froze. That was what was wrong with the room. It wasn't an adult room, it was a child's room. She thought of the toy catalog down on the hall table, and suddenly she knew that the missing piece of furniture, the one that would replace the cheap, plain bed, was a crib.

Stormy had planned a nursery.

Mae sank onto the bed, overwhelmed with sympathy for her. Stormy wasn't deep, but she was human and female and she'd loved Armand and wanted his child. And she'd planned her dreams in this room. Mae closed her eyes and pictured Stormy and a little redheaded daughter in this room, and she knew instinctively that Stormy had done the same.

When she couldn't bear it anymore, she went out of the room and closed the door and crossed to the room opposite it.

It was an adult room, decorated in browns and reds and dominated by a heavy mahogany bed. The only incongruous note was a large wastebasket full of socks and underwear beside the bed. Harold had packed clothes for Goodwill but had evidently drawn the line at passing on anything too personal.

Mae sat down on the bed feeling like Goldilocks. The first room had been too young, and this one was too old. She was due to hit the one that was just right next.

The only bed she could think of that would be just right was Mitch's.

She glanced at the clock on the nightstand. She'd been there two hours. It was time to move before someone found her. A cab was out of the question, but a bus was a possibility. She picked up her purse to look for money, only then remembering that she'd handed it all over to Mitch the night before for gas.

She opened the drawer beside the bed and checked for spare change, but Harold had been thorough, as always. The drawer was empty, and she was going to have to walk it.

She looked down at her feet and tried to remember how far it was to Mitch's. She didn't mind the hike, but her leather flats weren't meant to travel that far. She was starting blisters from just the first six miles. Mitch's place had to be another fifteen or twenty miles. Four or five hours. She'd be lame for life.

She threw her purse on the bed and went to check the boxes that Harold had packed for Goodwill. Maybe there would be shoes, even house slippers. Even five pairs of socks would be better than her leather flats. She pawed through the boxes, finally finding a pair of brand-new men's sneakers. She pulled them out and felt a pang of sorrow. Stormy had probably bought them for Armand, not knowing he'd never wear anything with a purple-and-magenta stripe. After seven years, she should have known, but Mae had a pretty good idea that Stormy had seen the Armand she'd wanted to see, not the real Armand. Stormy's Armand wanted a child and running shoes. The real Armand wanted Barbara Ross and money.

Poor Stormy.

A car door slammed out front and Mae froze, but after a moment she heard the front door of the next town house bang. She breathed out a long sigh of relief and scrambled to her feet. Now all she needed was socks. She went to the wastebasket and began to pull out socks, looking for the thickest pairs she could find. She was going to need about four pairs to get those shoes to fit her feet.

She was pulling out the fourth pair, when her hand struck something hard. She froze and then turned the wastebasket over to dump everything onto the floor.

There in the middle of the tangle of socks and undershorts was a brown leather book.

Mae's hands shook as she picked it up and turned it so she could see the spine—Lewis and the current year. She clutched it to her for a moment, and then the irony of the situation dawned on her. She'd finally found the diary, so the money was protected, but now there wasn't any money. She started to laugh, and then she pulled herself together. At least the diary might tell her where Armand had put the money. In the meantime, she had to get away. Now. She put the diary in her purse, put on the four pairs of socks that made her feet fit Armand's shoes, and five minutes later walked out of the back door of the town house and down the street to Overlook.

It was the first time in her life that she'd ever thought of Overlook as a safe place.

MITCH TRIED the art institute, Claud's, the storage place, Stormy's condo and finally Armand's town house, squelching every panicked vision of Mae being run down, shot, stabbed, smothered, poisoned, strangled, pushed under a train and arrested. Arrested was looking pretty good by the time he got to it, but it still wasn't what he wanted for Mae. What he wanted for Mae was for her to be with him, with his arms around her. After that, he would wing it, but her being with him was not negotiable. It was now top on his list of needs, and he felt more and more out of control the more he tried to find her and couldn't.

He even finally called Gio's, only to be met by alternating threats of violence and pleas to tell them where she was. Wherever she was, she wasn't at Gio's.

At nine that night, he turned toward home. He wasn't giving up, he'd search all night if he had to, he was not going to leave her alone in the dark, but first he was going home to try to regroup. He'd tried all the logical places; now he was going to have to do some fast thinking on the illogical ones.

The night was hot, beyond hot, and he rolled down the car window and drove through the city, trying to ignore the whine of police sirens and the screech of cars stopping too fast and the laughter of women that sounded like screams. His heart was so swollen with fear that it filled his chest, pressing on his lungs so that he couldn't breathe deeply enough, and his breath came in shallow sighs.

Please, God, let me find her, he prayed. *I'll never ask for anything again. Just let me find her and let her be all right.*

MAE SAT exhausted on Mitch's bed and watched the sky slowly turn gold, then orange, then purple, then blue-black through the single window of his apartment. She'd been drenched in sweat by the time she'd found his place, checked on the mailboxes in the hall for his apartment number and climbed through the window on the fire escape. She'd stripped immediately and showered, putting on one of his shirts because it was loose and cool and because it was the closest thing she could get to him, but within minutes she was drenched in sweat again, so she'd crawled onto the bed and sat there motionless, trying to think, trying not to fall asleep. The heat hung in the air, and his shirt stuck to her body, glued there with sweat, but she didn't notice. All through the late afternoon, she'd sifted through the snarl of facts and theories and fears that clogged her dazed mind, paging through the diary, trying to find the end of the knot, the one thing that would help her unravel the tangle her life had been fouled into. She'd found some fascinating things in the diary, but her basic situation remained the same: someone was trying to kill her, the police were after her and she was alone.

As the afternoon faded to evening and then to night, a new knot formed: Mitch should have been back by now. Wherever he was, whatever he was doing, it was past nine, and he should have been back by now.

What if he was hurt?

What if he was dead?

What if the shots hadn't been aimed at her? What if the shooter was aiming at Mitch?

What if he'd found him?

Carlo had been headed for jail the last time she'd seen him, but he'd be out by now. Uncle Gio's lawyers had getting Carlo out down to a science. Suppose he'd decided to put an end to Mitch's involvement with her. Suppose he'd decided to put an end to Mitch.

Mae leaned her head back against the iron bedstead and closed her eyes and concentrated on not panicking. She was fine alone. She could handle anything alone. She didn't need Mitch to get her out of trouble.

But she did need him.

She drew a ragged breath at the realization. She needed him in her life, not because he could protect her, or support her, or even put his arms around her.

She needed him because she loved him.

And suddenly she was terrified that she was never going to see him again. It didn't matter that he was a terrible relationship risk, that he was never going to be able to commit to her, that she was asking to get kicked in the emotional teeth by loving him. Those things were all logical and true and had nothing to do with love. Love had its own truth; you knew when you were in it and the likelihood of the success or failure of it had nothing to do with the fact of it.

At that moment, all she needed was to know that he was safe. That would be enough. She didn't need him to hold her or to save her. Just let him be all right. Somewhere. He didn't even have to be with her, he just had to be all right.

Then she heard a key scrape in the lock, and he came into the dark room, and she said, "Oh, thank God," and her voice was like a prayer.

"Mae?" In the gloom, she could see him stop and lean against the door, which closed under his weight. "Mae?"

"I'm here."

He drew a deep, uneven breath and said in a shaky attempt at lightness, "I've been looking for you, Mabel."

"I've been here," she said, trying to match his tone. "I figured you were with a librarian."

He came over and sat on the bed, and it sagged under his weight, tipping her toward him. He put his hand against her cheek and just sat there for a moment, touching her, and she closed her eyes because it felt so good to have him close, to feel his hand on her face, to know that he was all right.

He sighed. "I almost lost my mind." His voice was shaky again. "I thought I'd lost you forever."

She reached out for him, putting her hand against his chest, curling her fingers to clutch his shirt. "I was so scared. I thought Carlo had killed you. All I wanted was to know that you were safe. I'm all right now that you're safe." To her horror, she started to cry from relief. "I'm all right. I just couldn't stand it, thinking you were—"

"I love you." He kissed her and stopped her words with the soft caress of his mouth, making her dizzy with relief and comfort and love. She put her arms around him, holding him hard against her to prove that he was really there, and he held her just as close, just as tightly. "From now on, we stay together," he whispered in her ear. "This was just too damn scary. From now on, you stay with me."

"That's really what you want?" she asked him, swallowing hard. "No more pipeline?"

He smiled in the dark, his lips moving against her cheek. "No more pipeline. I've lost all my interest in the West. The only thing I want to explore is you."

"You wouldn't lie to me, would you?" she asked, and he said, "Everybody lies, Mabel. Everybody but us."

She nodded against his chest, too overwhelmed with relief and love to say anything else, and he kissed her again, deeper this time, and she melted into him, trying to merge with him so they'd never be apart again. He slipped his hand under her shirt, stroking his fingers up her damp back, holding her to him, and she pressed her lips to his neck, breathing him into her. "Make love to me," she whispered. "I want to be part of you."

He held her tighter for a moment, and then he said, "You're already part of me."

She stood up to pull his shirt over her head, breathing heavily in the heat that filled the room like fog, watching him gaze up at her in the blue light from the window. The shirt stuck to her, and she had to peel it off her sweat-slicked skin. She saw him stand then, too, the breadth of his body like a wall between her and whatever lay outside the door, and she heard him breathe deeper as he took off his shirt. She crawled back onto the bed and leaned forward to kiss his chest, licking at his salty dampness, and he stripped off his pants and then pulled her down on the bed with him, hot and damp and solid and safe.

She held him for a moment, savoring the warmth and weight of his body against hers, both of them slippery with sweat and heat and remembered fear and growing desire.

"It's almost enough just to hold you." He wrapped his arms tighter around her. "I'm just so damn glad that I'm holding you again."

She stretched against him, clutching him closer, trying to melt into him, dissolve her flesh into his, and he said, "Almost enough," and rolled his hips against hers. The heat flared low in her, and she bit him hard on the shoulder as he slid his fingers down her slippery body and into her, and she clenched around him, her tongue licking across his collarbone as she breathed into the waves of pleasure he stroked inside her.

They moved against each other slowly, rediscovering in deliberate detail what they'd found in tumbling haste the night before. The heat kept them slippery with need, salty with desire, and what had crashed and exploded before built slowly, inexorably, in low, swelling waves this time, moving higher and tighter, and when he finally arched himself into her and she enclosed him, they stopped for a moment, not breathing, listening to the lap of the blood in their veins, feeling the pulse where they were joined together and the throb of each other's hearts.

"I love you," Mae whispered to him, her lips moving on his. "I will love you forever."

His lips traced a silent echo on hers, and then all thought faded, and they were only rhythm and flesh and friction and heat and finally fusion, mindlessly one. And when all thought and fear and relief had been burned away, they slid wordlessly into sleep, still locked in each other's arms.

MITCH WOKE the next morning when she moved away from him, and he reached for her to pull her back against him.

"I need a shower." She kissed him and then slipped away, so Mitch shrugged and followed her.

It was a long shower.

"You know, if we do this often, we're going to have to start getting up earlier," Mae told him later as she went through his cupboards. "Why don't you have any food?"

"Because I never eat here. There are cockroaches the size of Bob here, and I don't want to encourage them."

Mae looked around warily.

Mitch sat on the edge of the bed. "Mabel, there have been some new developments."

"I know." Mae leaned on the counter. "I think I'm under arrest."

"I've got that handled. We're going to go see Nick right now, and he'll take care of everything."

Mae swallowed. "Okay. That sounds good."

Mitch hesitated. "There've been a few . . . updates on the situation."

Mae closed her eyes. "Hit me with them."

"Well, the good news is, you're not broke. The bad news is that your Uncle Armand embezzled your trust fund and then wrote in the diary that someone was forcing him to pay it all back. He deposited eight million in your account in the past three months. That's a motive for killing him."

Mae frowned. "The police think I was leaning on him? I didn't even know he'd done it."

Mitch blinked at her. "Mabel, did you miss the part about the eight million?"

"No." Mae walked over to the bed, and Mitch spared a moment to enjoy watching her move. He was going to spend the rest of his life watching her move. It was enough to make a man enthusiastic.

She picked up her purse and pulled out one of Armand's diaries. "Look what I found at the town house."

Mitch took it, read the date on the spine and gaped at her. "I searched that town house. Harold searched that town house."

Mae nodded. "I think somebody left it there to be found. Just not by me. Probably by the police. There are pages missing at the end, but there was enough there for me to figure out he'd put a lot of money back into my fund and into several other funds he'd looted. He was really unhappy about it because he'd worked it so there was no legal redress unless he confessed, which of course he did in the diary. He must have thought he was invincible."

"That sounds like our Armand." Mitch opened the diary and flipped through it. "Who made him put back the money?"

"Claud. Once he found out what Armand had done, he leaned hard on Armand to put it all back before the Lewis name got any more tarnished. It must have been Claud on the phone that night, making sure Armand had restored the accounts he'd looted. It's all in the diary." Mae laughed shortly. "Poor Uncle Claud. He finally forces Armand to pay everything back and gets everything covered up, and he even gets a bonus when Armand dies and won't be letting down the family anymore, and then we come along making noise about the diary." Mae sat down beside him. "No wonder he was willing to pay a fortune to get you out of the picture. He had everything taken care of, and there you were, screwing things up. That's what he meant that night when the lawyer told us there was nothing. Remember, he said, 'You and June and Harold will be taken care of'? He meant the money was back in the trust fund."

"Why didn't he just *tell* you that?"

"Uncle Claud doesn't tell people things. He takes care of things for them."

"When do you get that fund?"

"My thirty-fifth birthday. Six weeks from now."

Mitch whistled. "Armand was cutting it pretty fine." He flipped to the part of the book where the writing stopped.

"Somebody's ripped out the last pages here. What did Armand do right before he died?"

Mae shrugged. "Married Barbara. Sold the house to Dalton. Slept with Stormy. Maybe they were all in it together."

Mitch grinned. "Barbara, Dalton and Stormy? Not a chance." His grin faded. "How about Claud, Gio and Carlo? They all had motives."

"No, they didn't." Mae sounded exasperated. "They didn't like him, but they didn't kill him."

"It's the only thing that explains all the stuff that's been going down," Mitch told her gently. "Look at the motives. Claud sees the family name disgraced and his reputation damaged. Gio gets swindled and broods about it for years on end. Carlo thinks Armand turned him in to the police."

"He did. It's in the diary. Armand thought it was funny."

"Armand wasn't too bright. Just look at what they've done since then. Claud tries to buy me off and then buys my building and has me evicted. Carlo kills my car. Gio makes threatening phone calls to my clients. They're the only ones doing this stuff, Mae. They must have been in it together."

"And they shot at us? They shot at me? I don't believe it."

"You were wearing my jacket," Mitch told her. "It was dark. Carlo would love to pick me off just on general principle, let alone if he thought I was getting close to the diary and his motive for killing Armand."

"I don't believe it." Mae's voice was stubborn. "I do not believe that they all clubbed together and murdered Armand. Forget it."

"Well then, there's also this." Mitch reached for his jacket and pulled out the 1952 diary. "This is the year June's son, Ronnie, was born."

Mae took it from him. "I don't get it."

"It was a thought I had the other day, after the condom hunt. If June got pregnant, and Armand wasn't happy about it, what would he have done?"

"Made her get an abortion." Mae began to leaf through the diary.

"And he tried. But she wouldn't. So he stopped sleeping with her, and then, to make sure it never happened again..."

Mae looked up from the book. "He had a vasectomy."

Mitch nodded. "That was my theory. And sure enough, it's in there. And then, because Stormy wanted kids, he wore condoms rather than tell her that he was sterile."

"Stormy poked the holes in the condoms."

"Right." Mitch stood up. "I'm not exactly sure what that means, but it means something."

"You think Stormy killed Armand because he didn't tell her he'd had a vasectomy?" Mae rolled her eyes. "Oh, come on."

"Somebody killed him. The police don't go looking for trouble. If they were ready to arrest you, they're sure Armand was murdered."

Mae shook her head tiredly. "Can we think about it after we've eaten?" She tossed the diary on the bed. "I'm starving. I haven't had anything to eat for more than twenty-four hours, and you're going to have to buy me breakfast because you took my last twenty last night for gas, which, by the way, is why I had to walk a hundred miles to get here."

"You have plenty of twenties," Mitch said, abandoning his argument for the time being. "Eight million worth."

"Not for another six weeks." Mae stood and wrapped her arms around his waist pulling him close. "Until then, I'm at your mercy. Give me my twenty back."

"If you want my money, you have to marry me for it." Mitch stopped when he saw the expression on her face.

"Marry?" Mae swallowed and let go of him. "What happened to the librarians? Opening the West? I'm not your type?"

"You've got to be kidding." Mitch shook his head in amazement. "We went over this last night. Haven't you been paying attention the last forty-eight hours? We're in a different place now."

Mae nodded. "I know. I know. It's just . . . I've known you a week. Exactly a week. And I'm under arrest. And I'm hungry. And . . ."

"Okay." Mitch leaned over and kissed her cheek. "You're right. I'll feed you, get you unarrested and then we can talk. But I'm not leaving you."

"What are you talking about?" Mae grabbed his shirtsleeve. "Of course you're not leaving me. Are you crazy? I'm not sure about marriage, but I'm sure about us. You must be nuts. Leave me? Not in this lifetime, buster."

Mitch started to laugh. "Then you're going to have to make an honest man out of me, Mabel." He pried her fingers off his sleeve. "Stay here. It would not be a good idea for the police to see you having breakfast with me before Nick shows up to take your hand. I'll get breakfast and bring it back."

"And my twenty," Mae prompted. "I hate being broke."

"Well, in your case, it's not permanent." Mitch picked up his keys. "Stay here. Don't open the door. Don't talk to strangers. Don't—"

"I'm starving to death." Mae collapsed back onto the bed. "But I'm being polite about it because I don't have any money so I am completely in your hands."

"I mean it, don't move." Mitch opened the door. "Unless somebody shoots at you."

"You know, my life has gotten so much more exciting since I met you."

She smiled at him, and Mitch had to take a deep breath before he could speak. "Did I mention that I love you?"

"No," Mae said. "Mention it often."

"Don't move," Mitch said. "I'll be right back." He hesitated for a moment, and then said, "Don't move" again, and left.

He had a terrible feeling that leaving her was a bad idea, he just wasn't sure why.

THE ATM WAS less than a block away, but Mitch covered the distance at a trot, anyway. He wanted to get Mae to Nick and then to the police so he could start tracking down the answers to his questions, even if he had to beat them out of somebody.

Especially if he had to beat them out of Carlo. And Gio. And Claud. And Dalton. He didn't think Dalton was guilty, but he wanted to hit him, anyway.

There was no one at the ATM, so Mitch slid his card in without looking around and punched in his password.

The machine beeped. "Access denied. Your account has been closed. Your card has been confiscated."

"What?" Mitch yelled at the machine. "It can't be . . ." His card had worked fine the day before. Who could have . . . ?

Mitch pounded the ATM machine because he couldn't get to the murderers. He'd had enough with the Big Three and their hobbies. Poisoning old men, beating up cars, shooting at Mae, destroying credit ratings . . .

Mitch's internal rant died on that last thought. Who the hell would try to kill him, and then get really mad and go after his credit card? What kind of master plan was that?

And then it dawned on him.

It wasn't a master plan.

It was three master plans.

"I'll be damned," Mitch said, and turned to go back to Mae, only to see Carlo standing behind him.

"No, you'll be dead," Carlo said, and hit him.

10

AN HOUR LATER, Mitch still wasn't back, and Mae faced facts: she was on her own. She'd spent most of the hour trying to decide how Armand's vasectomy fit with the holes in the condoms, only belatedly realizing that Mitch wasn't going to show up.

The possibilities of what had happened were limited.

One was that Mitch had gotten tired of the whole mess and had washed his hands of her. It was what a prudent man would do, but Mitch wasn't prudent and he loved her. Not in a million years would he desert her.

Another was that Carlo had given up beating up on Mitch's car and had decided to beat directly on Mitch. This had the beauty of plausibility and previous attempts to recommend it, but even Carlo would have gotten tired of hitting him in an hour. If it had been just Carlo, Mitch would have been back by now. That theory was out, too.

A third theory was that the police had picked him up for questioning. If that was true, Mitch would stay away for a while to keep them away from her, but sooner or later, he'd have to come home. If they followed him and found her here, he'd be in trouble as an accomplice. That would be bad.

And then there was always the possibility that Armand really had been murdered, and the murderer had jumped Mitch and killed him.

Mae really hated that one, so she opted for number three, which meant that the smartest thing she could do was get out of the apartment in spite of Mitch's instructions. Waiting around for the police to follow Mitch home had no appeal whatsoever.

She picked up her purse and set out for the only place in Riverbend where she might possibly be safe.

She had a phone call to make.

WHEN MITCH CAME TO, he found himself looking up at the severed head of Holofernes in Gio's office. It didn't seem like a good omen. Then he turned his head and saw his three least favorite people in the world.

"Ah, Mr. Peatwick, with us at last," Claud said from his vantage point in a nearby chair.

"Where's Mae Belle?" Gio demanded from behind his desk.

"I'm gonna kill you next time," Carlo promised, looming over him.

Mitch reached up and touched his temple, and his hand came away bloody. He groaned and eased himself slowly to his feet, tottering as he stood, and then, as Carlo smirked at him for being such a wimp, Mitch sucker-punched him to the floor.

"That's for hitting Harold," Mitch told him as he did the looming this time. "I still owe you for shooting my car, clubbing me on the head and almost killing Mae."

Carlo surged to his feet, and Mitch drew back his fist, and Gio yelled, *"Wait."*

Carlo and Mitch both froze.

"He almost killed Mae?" Gio turned his little obsidian eyes on Carlo. "What did you do?"

"Nothin'." Carlo stuck out his jaw. "He's lying. I wouldn't hurt Mae. Ever."

"You couldn't see her," Mitch said. "That night at the storage shed, you were shooting at her not me. You came within an inch of killing her, you moron."

"Is this true?" Gio's eyes impaled his grandson. "Did you do this thing?"

"I shot at him." Carlo's face was mulish. "I never shot at Mae."

"He missed her by a couple of inches," Mitch told Gio. "He thought he was shooting at me because she was wearing my jacket, but he almost killed her." He shook his head. "You know, giving him a gun is not a good idea."

"No more guns," Gio said to Carlo who glared at Mitch. "I want them all."

"You might want to take the knives away from him, too," Mitch suggested. "There was that incident with the finger...."

"You stay out of this," Gio snapped, and Mitch said, "No."

Gio surged up out of his desk chair. "Nobody says no to me—"

"Well, they do now," Mitch told him. "I've had it with all three of you. Who do you think you are, anyway? All of you, yapping away about how you want to protect Mae, and then you do everything you can to get her arrested or, God knows, killed. The police are after her, a murderer is on the loose and you take out the only guy who's protecting her." He jerked his thumb at his chest. "Me."

Claud stirred in his chair. "There is no murderer, and we know about the police. We've retained a lawyer. Now, if you'll—"

"She doesn't need your lawyer," Mitch said, exasperated. "I got her a lawyer. She's got everything she needs except me, and the only reason I'm not with her is because you guys think you're in a *Godfather* movie."

"She doesn't need your cheap shyster," Gio began.

Mitch turned on him. "He's not cheap. He's going to cost you a friggin' fortune. I was going to cover it, but after this last trick you pulled, he's going to bill you."

Claud narrowed his eyes, which made them essentially disappear. "And why would we pay for this lawyer?"

"Because I finally figured out what the hell was going on here," Mitch said. "And you are in deep trouble, all of you."

"Where is Mae Belle?" Gio demanded.

Mitch felt his temper hit boiling and tried hard to keep the lid on it. "Well, she was at my place, but knowing Mabel, she's hit the road by now, so I have no idea where she is, and that's your fault, too, Grandpa, so don't hassle me about it. You know, I could have figured out this whole thing a lot sooner if you hadn't been playing your dumb Master of the Universe games."

"Aside from Carlo's assaults, there is nothing—"

Mitch swung around to glare down at him. "Oh, no you don't, Claud. You're in this as deep as he is. You should never have messed with my credit, Claud. Bad move."

"What credit?" Gio scowled. "Who gives a damn about your credit? I want—"

"Forget it." Mitch leaned over the edge of the desk and stared him down. "What you want doesn't matter anymore. Mae's been arrested for murder, which means somebody actually did kill Armand."

"Nonsense." Claud dismissed him without a flicker of emotion. "You're just protecting your job."

Mitch took a deep breath. "Claud, pay attention here. The police *arrested* Mae. They don't do that because they're bored. They do that because they think they can get a conviction. If there was any doubt at all that Armand had been murdered, they wouldn't be arresting Mae. Trust me on this."

Claud stared at him as if Mitch had crawled out from under a rock, but he didn't say anything.

"I was pulling for you three as the killers because I could spare all of you without too much trouble. But I couldn't make it work." Mitch glared down at Carlo. "Carlo was stupid enough to slash my tires—" Carlo growled and Mitch braced himself for another punch "—but he wasn't smart enough or rich enough or connected enough to get me evicted from my office." Carlo stayed put, and Mitch turned to Claud. "Claud could get me evicted, but he wouldn't threaten my clients with physical danger." Mitch then faced the apoplectic little man behind the desk. "And Gio would threaten his own mother, but he wouldn't bother with shooting my car. I liked the idea that the three of you were in this together, but Mae said no, and eventually even I couldn't see any of you trusting the others with cab fare, let alone a murder plot."

"I don't get this, and I don't care," Gio said. "I want—"

"Then Mae was arrested and somebody killed my credit. And right there at the ATM, I was hit by the solution. And then fifteen seconds later, I was hit by Carlo." Suddenly overcome by disappointment, Mitch stared at Carlo. "You will never know how much I wanted you to be the bad guy in this. Ohio has the death penalty, you know."

"Mr. Peatwick, we're really uninterested in your credit rating," Claud said. "We want—"

"Then why did you kill it, Claud? I should be grateful because that's what made me finally catch on. I mean, two nights ago, somebody tries to shoot us, and that doesn't work, so somebody gets Mae arrested for murder, and th doesn't work, so then this guy escalates the battle and goes after my *credit card?*" Mitch shook his head. "I know your Dun and Bradstreet is more important to you than your prostate, but even you must have figured out that losing my credit card would run a poor second to getting shot. That's when I knew I was dealing with more than one loon."

"Do you realize to whom you are speaking?" Claud asked him coldly.

"Yeah." Mitch stared him down, just as coldly. "I'm talking to the guy who ruined my credit rating. That would be you, and that's illegal. Financial harassment. I discussed this with my attorney when you had me evicted, and he says it should be an interesting lawsuit."

Claud dismissed him with a wave of his hand. "No attorney would touch a lawsuit like that."

"Mine would. He likes Bolivian tin mines and redheaded radicals. He lives for risk."

"Some ambulance chaser." Claud chuckled derisively. It sounded like a death rattle. "Some nobody."

"Nick Jamieson." Mitch watched the smile fade from Claud's face. "Yeah, he's good, isn't he? Well, look on the bright side, he's defending Mabel, too."

"How do you know Nick Jamieson?" Claud demanded.

"I'm his stockbroker." Mitch watched Claud blink as he absorbed the information and then Mitch turned to Gio. "Then there's you. Threatening my clients, harassing my landlord, making nasty phone calls. You ought to be ashamed. Especially since the cops would love to get something on you. You really screwed up this time, Gio. And then there's my personal favorite, the bottom feeder in your gene pool." He turned to glare at Carlo. "You owe me twelve new tires, new seats, all new windshields and lights, and a hell of a lot of bodywork. I can't believe you beat up my car like that."

Gio pounded on his desk. "Will you forget that damn car? I don't care about the car. I will pay for the car, and this lawyer, and anything else. Just tell me, where the hell is Mae Belle?"

"I don't know, Gio." Mitch stood up straight again. "My guess is, she's gone to see the murderer. I'm a little concerned about that. And that's why I'm leaving now."

Carlo blocked his way. "You're not going anywhere."

Mitch faced him. "I will go around you, over you, or through you, whatever it takes. But I am going to Mae."

And then he walked toward Carlo and the door.

MAE LET HERSELF in the front door of the town house at the same time that Stormy came down the stairs carrying a suitcase.

They both stopped, surprised.

"I was just going to call you." Mae eyed the suitcase. "Going somewhere?"

"South America. I just came by for my passport." Stormy put the suitcase down, frowning as if she'd had a sudden thought. "I thought you'd been arrested."

"Now, why would you think that?" Mae tossed her purse on the table.

Stormy blinked. "I heard it on the radio."

"No, you didn't. We've had the radio on all morning. No escaped socialites." Mae sat on the edge of the table and looked at her sadly. "You framed me, didn't you, Stormy?"

Stormy bit her lip. "It wouldn't have stuck. Your uncles would have gotten every lawyer in Riverbend."

"Why did you do it?"

Stormy shrugged. "You were the one who started the murder rumor. I figured it made sense that you'd be guilty."

"No. I mean why did you kill Armand?"

Stormy opened her eyes wide. "I didn't."

Mae shook her head. "You're good, sweetheart, but that wide-eyed bit went out with Brigid."

"Who's Brigid?" Stormy asked with genuine confusion this time.

"You killed him because you loved him, didn't you?" Mae tried to keep the sympathy out of her voice. After all, this woman was a killer.

Just not a cold-blooded one.

Stormy snorted. "Why would I love him? He was a mean old man. And I'd have been stupid to kill him. He'd already given me all the money I was going to get. I wasn't in his will. I—"

"You loved him, and he was going to leave you. You tried to keep him by getting pregnant. That's why you poked holes in all of his condoms." She looked at Stormy sadly. "That wouldn't have worked, you know. He never gave a damn about kids. Not about Ronnie and not about me."

"If somebody put a hole in a condom, it was Armand." Stormy stuck her chin out. "He wanted me to stay with him after he got married. Maybe he thought if I got pregnant, I'd have to stay."

"He had a vasectomy in 1952." Mae watched Stormy's face go white.

"He couldn't have." She sounded as if she was out of breath. "He promised me—"

"He promised a lot of people a lot of things he had no intention of delivering." Mae saw Stormy lift her chin in defense, and she felt an ache of pity for her. "I'm sorry, Stormy. It's in his diary. Right after June told him she was pregnant, he had it done. He was never going to give you a baby."

"Then why did we always use condoms?" Stormy flared. "If—"

"To convince you he might give you a baby someday. He lied to you, Stormy. He lied to you to keep you, and then he dumped you for Barbara's money." Mae watched the younger woman totter to a chair. "He told you Monday night that he was married, didn't he? Is that when he told you it was all over?"

"No." Stormy straightened her shoulders. "No. I read it in his diary. It was just like always. He poured himself a big brandy and put it on the night table, and then he took a shower, and I read his diary to find out what was going on."

"You read his private journal?"

"Not all the time," Stormy said defensively. "Just when I wanted to know what was going on. Armand didn't tell me much. And I read in it that he'd married her. I couldn't believe it. It was awful. And I knew if I said anything, he'd leave." She sniffed. "Armand didn't like it when I asked him stuff."

Mae sank into the nearest chair. "You were with him seven years, and he wouldn't let you ask him stuff?"

Stormy nodded. "After a while, it got on my nerves, you know? And Armand said I was high-strung and got his doctor to prescribe some pills for me. And he was right. After I took a pill, I really wasn't interested in asking him stuff or having things my way."

Mae closed her eyes. He'd kept her stoned on tranquilizers. "Good old Armand, always looking out for other people."

"So I decided that I'd put one of my pills in his brandy so he'd stay calm and talk to me," Stormy said matter-of-factl "I put one on the night table and smacked it with my high heel, and then I brushed the pieces into his brandy, but it didn't look like very much, so I smacked another one. And then I thought about him leaving me, and I smacked another one, and then I sort of lost count."

"You laced his brandy with tranquilizers?" Mae swallowed.

Stormy nodded. "And when he came out of the shower, he drank it, and then I told him I knew he was married, and that he was going to have to divorce her. And he told me not to be stupid, that he was never going to leave me. He was just going to be married to her and keep me on the side. It was like Medea."

"Medea?" Mae said, startled. "Medea who?"

"You know, Medea." Stormy frowned at her. "The Greek woman who was married to Jason. Armand and I saw Diana Rigg play her in New York two years ago. It was really something."

"How does Medea—"

"Jason dumped her for another woman, and then told her that he was doing it for her and the kids." Stormy laughed, a short, lonely sound in the stillness of the room. "Armand said he was doing it for us, for him and me."

Mae sighed. "He was doing it for him. He was broke and wanted her money."

Stormy waved away the idea. "Armand wasn't broke. Armand was rich."

"Armand was tapped out, stone broke," Mae said firmly. "It's all gone. The house, the furniture, the car . . . he sold everything and gave it to you and me, and then married Barbara for a new start on a fortune."

"That's why he married her?" Stormy's voice cracked with stunned disbelief. "That's why?"

"That's why." Mae hesitated. "I'm really sorry, Stormy. You deserved better."

After a moment, Stormy nodded. "Yeah. I did."

They sat silent for a moment, and then Mae asked, "How did he die?"

Stormy swallowed back the tears that were brightening her eyes. "I told him I had the diary. I told him he couldn't have it back unless he divorced her. And he got really mad and yelled at me and drank all the brandy at once, and then pretty soon he got really sleepy, and I thought he was just going to sleep, so I lay down next to him and . . ." She stopped, her lower lip quivering.

"And he fell asleep and died." Mae closed her eyes. "It must have been a shock when he stopped breathing."

"Yeah." Stormy nodded mournfully. "That's when I called Claud. And then I cried." She sniffed. "I really did love him."

"I know." Mae spared a thought for the poetic justice of Armand's death and then jerked her head at Stormy's suitcase. "You still leaving?"

Stormy sniffed once more and stood up. "Yeah. My flight's in an hour, and I got a ride coming." She smiled woefully at Mae. "Are you going to try and stop me?"

"No." The truth was, Stormy had about as much chance of escaping as she did of flying without the plane. She might get away for a week or a month, but they'd find her sooner or later. Stormy was never going to be able to take care of herself.

Stormy watched her, her uncertainty palpable. "I didn't kill him on purpose, you know."

"I know." Mae stood up to face her. "Look, I'm not going to be judge and jury here, and I'm sure not going to call the police. They'd just come and arrest me."

Stormy was still wary. "So I can just leave?"

"Yes."

"Okay." The buzzer rang, and Stormy picked up her suitcase and her purse. "That's my ride. I gotta go." She hesitated. "I always liked you, you know?"

"Thank you."

"The only reason I pinned it on you was that I knew you'd get off."

Mae fought down the urge to be caustic. "I appreciate that."

The buzzer rang again.

"Well, good luck," Stormy said.

"Good luck," Mae echoed sadly.

Stormy waved at her halfheartedly and opened the door.

"Hello, Stormy." Mitch looked over her shoulder at Mae. "We were just looking for Mabel, and there she is. Could we talk to you for a minute?" He took Stormy's arm and walked her back into the room, closely followed by Claud, Gio and Carlo.

Stormy went with him, dropping her suitcase by the door.

"What is this, a parade?" Mae scowled at them, annoyed at the interference. Then she saw the bloody bruise on Mitch's forehead. "What happened to you?"

Mitch let go of Stormy and went to her. "Your entire lunatic family kidnapped me and refused to let me go, so I brought them along."

"Oh, Mitch, I'm sorry." Mae touched his temple lightly.

He closed her hand in his. "It's okay."

Mae squeezed his hand and then dropped it to return to her current problem. She had to get Stormy out of there. "Look, Stormy has to leave—"

"No, she doesn't," Mitch said.

"Yes, she does," Stormy said, and Mae turned to her and looked straight down the barrel of the small gun Stormy was holding on her. "I've got nothing against Mae, but I know she's the only one you all care about. So if anybody tries anything, I'll have to shoot her."

Mitch met Mae's eyes. "You know, nothing has gone the way I planned it today," he said.

No MATTER HOW he looked at it, things were bad. He was trapped with at least two homicidal maniacs, one of whom had a gun pointed at the head of the woman he loved. If he could only convince Stormy to shoot Carlo, life would be perfect, but that was a long shot.

The short shot was to Mae's head.

Think fast. "You know, Stormy, we can get you a good lawyer. We had one for Mae, but he's adaptable. We'll just white out her name on all the legal stuff he's drawn up for her and write yours in."

"If you hurt Mae, I'll kill you," Carlo said to Stormy.

Mitch rolled his eyes in exasperation. "Shoot him, will you? I, for one, will swear it was self-defense."

"Shut up, all of you." Stormy's eyes went to stare at Carlo warily, and Mitch immediately took two steps to the right so that he was standing between Mae and the gun.

"What are you doing?" Mae poked at his back, trying to see around him.

Mitch put his hand behind him to keep her in place. "Listen, if I wasn't almost positive that she probably wouldn't shoot, I wouldn't be doing this."

"I thought you had needs." Mae sounded a little breathless.

"I did. I do." Mitch took a deep breath himself as he watched Stormy and her wobbly gun hand. "It's just that the top of my list has changed."

"Oh."

Mitch felt her rest her head between his shoulder blades for a minute. "Are you all right?"

"Yes, I will," Mae said.

"Will what?"

"Yes, I will marry you." He felt her arms go around his waist from behind. "I will definitely marry you."

"Mae!" Carlo howled, and Stormy moved the gun to him.

Mitch tried to disentangle her arms from around him so he could move them both out of gun range if he had to. "Could we discuss this later?"

"Sure." She held him tighter. "I just wanted to go on record in case one of us gets shot and dies."

"Nobody's going to get shot." Mitch tried to hold Stormy's eyes with his. "Shooting someone would be bad, even if it was Carlo. We're all going to be fine."

"I love you," Mae said.

"I'm gonna kill you," Carlo snarled at Mitch and lunged at him, and Stormy squeaked and jumped back, and the gun went off and shot Carlo in the leg.

Carlo went down with one short scream, Gio dropped to his knees beside him and the buzzer rang.

"That's my ride." Stormy motioned Gio to the door. "Get up and get that, please. And don't try anything funny, or I'll . . . I'll shoot you, too." Then she looked at Carlo. "I'm really sorry. You scared me. You shouldn't have moved."

Gio put his hand on Carlo's shoulder.

"I'm okay, Grandpa," Carlo said through gritted teeth, and Mitch felt some respect for him for the first time. He didn't have any personal experience with getting shot, but he knew that it had to hurt like hell.

Gio stood and opened the door.

"I have the tickets, my dove," Newton said as he came in, and then he stopped at the tableau before him. "What's this? A bon voyage party?" He went to stand next to Stormy and nodded to Mae. "You must be Mabel. I'm very pleased to be meeting you at last."

"Likewise," Mae said faintly.

"Newton," Mitch said. "Could we discuss this?"

"No!" Stormy's voice was the firmest he'd ever heard it. "We have to leave now," she said to Newton. She leaned into him slightly, and Mitch watched him close his eyes.

"So you'll have to tie them up," Stormy went on.

Newton nodded.

Mitch sighed. He hoped Newton liked South America because coming back north was not going to be an option.

Then Newton stepped behind Stormy and jerked her gun hand up. She fired the gun once into the ceiling before he could get it away from her, and then he had it in his hand.

"Newton?" she cried, and he shook his head at her.

"I'm not going to play the sap for you, sweetheart," he told her.

Mae pushed her way around Mitch to go to Carlo. "Newton, you bastard," she said on her way past him. "I can't believe you betrayed the woman you love."

Newton shrugged. "It's a tough world, Mabel." He transferred his attention to Gio who was now standing again, satisfied that Carlo was all right. "Open the door and wave your handkerchief out there. It's a signal for the police."

"The police?" Stormy's knees gave out, and she sat down on the floor as Gio went to the door, strangely obedient as he cast anxious glances at his grandson.

"It's okay." Newton patted Stormy on the head as if she were a puppy. "Your lawyer's meeting you at the police station."

Mitch gaped at him. "You got her a lawyer already?"

"Well, of course." Newton blinked as if anything else was unthinkable. "I called Nick before I called the police." He smiled down at Stormy. "I told him he'd be defending a beautiful woman who killed her lover in a crime of passion."

Stormy rolled her eyes and put her head in her hands.

"And what did he say?" Mitch asked, fascinated.

"He said, 'Mae shot Mitch?'"

"Don't think I haven't thought about it," Mae said from her place beside Carlo, and then the town house was full of police, and someone called for an ambulance.

Fifteen minutes later, Stormy and Newton were gone, and the paramedics had Carlo strapped onto a stretcher, and the party was definitely over.

"Wait a minute," Mae said, and they all stopped, paramedics included. "I just want to make this perfectly clear, right now, before we all leave." She pointed to Mitch. "I am marrying this man."

Claud turned to Mitch. "I'll ruin you financially."

Gio glared at Mitch. "I'll ruin you professionally."

Carlo struggled to sit up on the stretcher while the paramedics held him down. "I'll *kill* you," he said to Mitch.

Mitch looked at all three of them with disgust. "You know, I never said yes. I might not even marry her. There are a lot of librarians out there that I've never—"

"Stop it." Mae's voice cut across all of them. "I'm marrying him. That's final. That's what I want."

All four of them gazed at her a moment and then turned to look at one another, and for just that moment, Mitch felt a bond with them.

He was now part of the whatever-Mae-Belle-wants team. In fact, he had been for some time now, watching out for her from the background like Claud, worrying about her incessantly like Gio, wanting her until he was crazy from it like Carlo.

He had met the enemy, and they were him.

Claud nodded at Mae and turned to him. "You'll sign a prenuptial."

Gio sighed at Mae and turned to him. "You'll bring her to dinner every Sunday."

Carlo swung his fist at Mitch and spat, "I'll kill you."

"No, you will not," Gio told him. "He's family now."

Carlo moaned and fell back onto the stretcher, and the relieved-looking paramedics carted him away, followed by Gio and Claud.

"This is awfully sudden," Mitch told Mae as she stared at him, daring him to try to get out of marrying her. "I need time to think about this. Maybe—"

"Do you love me?" Mae demanded.

"More than life itself," Mitch said.

Mae swallowed. "Really?"

"Really." Mitch smiled down at her. "I know. Surprised the hell out of me, too."

She stepped closer to him and put her arms around him, resting her forehead against his chest. "I'm really hungry, and I'm really tired, but mostly I'm just so glad that you're safe and I'm with you that I can't stand it."

"It's all right now," Mitch told her, holding her, his cheek against her hair. "It really is all right now. It's all over. Except for us. We're never going to be over."

"I love you," Mae said into his jacket. "I don't want to spend another day without you."

Mitch's arms tightened around her. "Well, if we can get Carlo neutered, you won't ever have to," he said.

Epilogue

BOB WAS BACK in Mitch's chair again.

"We've discussed this," Mitch said, glaring at the dog. "Get down."

Bob looked at him woefully. Looking woeful was his new stock-in-trade. Now that he was living in a house where the counters didn't remind him of steak, he'd stopped beating his brains out on the furniture and had taken to sitting on it instead, doing a nice imitation of an abused dog. His sense of being displaced no doubt came in part because his new brothers and sister, Maurice, George II and Carmen, all newly liberated from the pound, were taking up floor space that Bob felt strongly should be his. *I have to sit up here,* his mournful eyes seemed to say. *You have dogs on the rest of the floor.* Secretly, however, Mitch knew Bob was jubilant. He could see it in the dog's eyes every time he caught him in the desk chair.

"Down," he said, and Bob sighed and jumped down and went to lie on the rug by the window, reproachful even as the breeze from the river blew the white gauze curtains across his back.

"Yeah, you have a hard life," Mitch jeered at him and sat down just as Mae came through the door. She said something, but Mitch was watching her move again and didn't catch it. "What?"

"I said, have you been yelling at Bob again?" She stooped to scratch the dog behind the ears. "He's very sensitive."

"He is not." Mitch turned on the computer on his desk to distract himself from the sight of his wife bending over. He never got anything done when she was around.

"June says lunch is in an hour and don't be late. Harold says the game is this afternoon and you may watch it in his room if you'd like, he doesn't care." Mae grinned at him. "He cares."

"I'll watch the game," Mitch promised. "I've just got to get this done—"

"Stormy wrote." Mae straightened and came toward him. "Another guard proposed. That's the third one in four months." She tossed the letter on the desk.

"I talked to Nick yesterday. He thinks she'll be out in a year."

Mae bit her lip. "That's a long time."

Mitch snorted. "Not for murder, it isn't. If it wasn't for Nick's pioneering use of the dumb-as-a-rock defense, she'd be in for a lot longer. Besides, Nick says she thinks it's fine. She's getting college credits, and she wants to be a sophomore when she gets out."

"Well, at least she's not with Armand anymore. Even prison has to be better than Armand. Has Newton been writing to her?"

"No." Mitch scowled at her. "And don't give him any ideas. He has enough on his hands trying to run the agency. He's still trying to make divorce work classy."

"Well, if anyone can do it, Newton can." Mae sat down on the edge of the desk. "Uncle Gio called. He said to come early on Sunday so you can get in some boccie ball before we eat."

"Only if Carlo doesn't play. I swear, the last six times he hit me with the ball were not accidents."

"You're just paranoid." Mae looked at him with palpable affection. "And besides, Uncle Gio loves to play with you."

"Why?" Mitch shook his head, dumbfounded. "I keep beating him. Why does he still want to play?"

"Because you beat him. Everybody else that he plays with lets him win."

"Why?"

"Because if they don't, he fires them."

Mitch started to laugh. "Your family is nuts."

"Not all of them." She hesitated and Mitch braced himself. "I talked to Uncle Claud this morning. He's been looking over the investments."

Mitch scowled. "Uncle Claud is an unadventurous old twit."

"He said you were doing brilliantly with them," Mae went on.

"But an astute old twit." Mitch looked up at her. "Does he still hate me?"

"Yes, but he's dealing with it." Mae patted his shoulder. "In fact, he had a suggestion. He thinks I should have a child."

"You do." Mitch turned his attention back to his computer. "Me."

"I mentioned that. He said you needed someone to play with."

"Good. Hire a French maid." When the silence stretched out, Mitch looked up again and grinned. "Forget pretending you're mad. I know you too well."

Mae gazed at him serenely. "If I ever find you with a French maid, I will hire an Italian bodyguard."

"You'd cheat on me with a bodyguard? I'm hurt."

"No, the bodyguard would take the maid away from you, and you'd come back to me." Mae smiled at him. "And then I'd make you pay."

Mitch laughed and pulled her into his lap. "I'm crazy about you, Mabel."

"Good." She snuggled deeper into his lap. "Let's make a baby."

"Right now?"

"Right now. I am ovulating as of this very minute." Mae batted her eyes at him. "Play your cards right, you could get lucky."

Mitch drew back from her a little. "How do you know that it's right this very minute?"

"I have a sixth sense about these things."

Mitch closed his eyes and thought of all the other things that Mae had wanted: the diary, the house on the river, the dogs . . . him. Those had all turned out well, Bob notwithstanding. And now a baby. He had a momentary vision of Mae staring down at a miniature Mae Belle, stubborn brown eyes meeting stubborn brown eyes. It was about time Mae met somebody she couldn't push around.

And he could watch.

He laughed, and she said, "What?" suspicion heavy in her voice, and he tipped her gently onto the floor, moving his hand up her thigh as his body covered hers.

"Here?" Mae grinned up at him as she twined her hands around his neck and eased her hips against his. "Right here on the floor in front of Bob? I'm shocked. I really am shocked." She unbuttoned his shirt as she spoke, and he shivered as her fingers trailed down his chest.

"Whatever you want, Mabel," Mitch said. "That's what you get."

Then he kissed her, and after a couple of minutes, since neither of them were paying him the slightest attention, Bob jumped back onto the desk chair and fell asleep.

HARLEQUIN® Temptation

Secret Fantasies

Do you have a secret fantasy?

America's sweetheart Josie Eastman does. She's always done what she's told, never endangered her precious career. And she's sick of it. So she drops everything and escapes into the arms of a bad-boy rancher. But soon she realizes why she was always told, "Never love a cowboy...." Enjoy #546 NEVER LOVE A COWBOY by Kate Hoffmann, available in July 1995.

Everybody has a secret fantasy. And you'll find them all in Temptation's exciting new yearlong miniseries, Secret Fantasies. Beginning January 1995, one book each month focuses on the hero and heroine's innermost romantic desires....

MOVE OVER, MELROSE PLACE!

> Apartment for rent
> One bedroom
> Bachelor Arms
> 555-1234

Come live and love in L.A. with the tenants of Bachelor Arms. Enjoy a year's worth of wonderful love stories and meet colorful neighbors you'll bump into again and again.

When Blythe Fielding planned her wedding and asked her two best friends, Caitlin and Lily, to be bridesmaids, none of them knew a new romance was around the corner for each of them—not even the bride! These entertaining, dramatic stories of friendship, mystery and love by JoAnn Ross continue the exploits of the residents of Bachelor Arms and answer one very important question: Will Blythe ever get to walk down the aisle? Find out in:

NEVER A BRIDE (May 1995) #537

FOR RICHER OR POORER (June 1995) #541

THREE GROOMS AND A WEDDING (July 1995) #545

Soon to move into Bachelor Arms are the heroes and heroines in books by always popular Candace Schuler and Judith Arnold. A new book every month!

Don't miss the goings-on at Bachelor Arms.

THREE GROOMS:
Case, Carter and Mike

TWO WORDS:
"We Don't!"

ONE MINISERIES:

GROOMS ON THE RUN

Starting in May 1995, Harlequin Temptation
brings you an exciting miniseries called

GROOMS ON THE RUN

Each book (and there'll be one a month for three
months!) features a sexy hero who's ready to say,
"I do!" but ends up saying, "I don't!"

Watch for these special Temptations:

In May, **I WON'T!** by Gina Wilkins #539
In June, **JILT TRIP** by Heather MacAllister #543
In July, **NOT THIS GUY!** by Glenda Sanders #547

Available wherever Harlequin books are sold.

PRIZE SURPRISE
SWEEPSTAKES
OFFICIAL ENTRY COUPON

This entry must be received by: JUNE 30, 1995
This month's winner will be notified by: JULY 15, 1995

YES, I want to win the Panasonic 31" TV! Please enter me in the drawing and let me know if I've won!

Name_____

Address _____ Apt. _____

City_____ State/Prov._____ Zip/Postal Code_____

Account #_____

Return entry with invoice in reply envelope.

© 1995 HARLEQUIN ENTERPRISES LTD.

CTV KAL

PRIZE SURPRISE
SWEEPSTAKES
OFFICIAL ENTRY COUPON

This entry must be received by: JUNE 30, 1995
This month's winner will be notified by: JULY 15, 1995

YES, I want to win the Panasonic 31" TV! Please enter me in the drawing and let me know if I've won!

Name_____

Address _____ Apt. _____

City_____ State/Prov._____ Zip/Postal Code_____

Account #_____

Return entry with invoice in reply envelope.

© 1995 HARLEQUIN ENTERPRISES LTD.

CTV KAL

OFFICIAL RULES

PRIZE SURPRISE SWEEPSTAKES 3448

NO PURCHASE OR OBLIGATION NECESSARY

Three Harlequin Reader Service 1995 shipments will contain respectively, coupons for entry into three different prize drawings, one for a Panasonic 31" wide-screen TV, another for a 5-piece Wedgwood china service for eight and the third for a Sharp ViewCam camcorder. To enter any drawing using an Entry Coupon, simply complete and mail according to directions.

There is no obligation to continue using the Reader Service to enter and be eligible for any prize drawing. You may also enter any drawing by hand printing the words "Prize Surprise," your name and address on a 3"x5" card and the name of the prize you wish that entry to be considered for (i.e., Panasonic wide-screen TV, Wedgwood china or Sharp ViewCam). Send your 3"x5" entries via first-class mail (limit: one per envelope) to: Prize Surprise Sweepstakes 3448, c/o the prize you wish that entry to be considered for, P.O. Box 1315, Buffalo, NY 14269-1315, USA or P.O. Box 610, Fort Erie, Ontario L2A 5X3, Canada.

To be eligible for the Panasonic wide-screen TV, entries must be received by 6/30/95; for the Wedgwood china, 8/30/95; and for the Sharp ViewCam, 10/30/95.

Winners will be determined in random drawings conducted under the supervision of D.L. Blair, Inc., an independent judging organization whose decisions are final, from among all eligible entries received for that drawing. Approximate prize values are as follows: Panasonic wide-screen TV ($1,800); Wedgwood china ($840) and Sharp ViewCam ($2,000). Sweepstakes open to residents of the U.S. (except Puerto Rico) and Canada, 18 years of age or older. Employees and immediate family members of Harlequin Enterprises, Ltd., D.L. Blair, Inc., their affiliates, subsidiaries and all other agencies, entities and persons connected with the use, marketing or conduct of this sweepstakes are not eligible. Odds of winning a prize are dependent upon the number of eligible entries received for that drawing. Prize drawing and winner notification for each drawing will occur no later than 15 days after deadline for entry eligibility for that drawing. Limit: one prize to an individual, family or organization. All applicable laws and regulations apply. Sweepstakes offer void wherever prohibited by law. Any litigation within the province of Quebec respecting the conduct and awarding of the prizes in this sweepstakes must be submitted to the Regies des loteries et Courses du Quebec. In order to win a prize, residents of Canada will be required to correctly answer a time-limited arithmetical skill-testing question. Value of prizes are in U.S. currency.

Winners will be obligated to sign and return an Affidavit of Eligibility within 30 days of notification. In the event of noncompliance within this time period, prize may not be awarded. If any prize or prize notification is returned as undeliverable, that prize will not be awarded. By acceptance of a prize, winner consents to use of his/her name, photograph or other likeness for purposes of advertising, trade and promotion on behalf of Harlequin Enterprises, Ltd., without further compensation, unless prohibited by law.

For the names of prizewinners (available after 12/31/95), send a self-addressed, stamped envelope to: Prize Surprise Sweepstakes 3448 Winners, P.O. Box 4200, Blair, NE 68009.

RPZ KAL